John Rector's short fiction has appeared in numerous magazines and won several awards, including the Porterhouse prize. His first novel, *The Grove*, was a bestselling e-book and is forthcoming from Pocket Books. He lives in Omaha, Nebraska and is currently working on his third novel, *The Clinic*.

You can read John Rector's blog at:
http://johnrector.blogspot.com.

cold kiss

JOHN RECTOR

POCKET
BOOKS

LONDON • SYDNEY • NEW YORK • TORONTO

First published in Great Britain by Pocket Books, 2010
An imprint of Simon & Schuster UK Ltd
A CBS COMPANY

1 3 5 7 9 10 8 6 4 2

Simon & Schuster UK Ltd
1st Floor
222 Gray's Inn Road
London WC1X 8HB

www.simonandschuster.co.uk

Simon & Schuster Australia
Sydney

A CIP catalogue record for this book is available from the British Library

ISBN: 978-1-84983-068-3

Typeset by Hewer Text UK Ltd, Edinburgh
Printed and bound in Great Britain by CPI Cox & Wyman,
Reading, Berkshire RG1 8EX

For Amy, of course

Freezing was not so bad as people thought.
There were lots worse ways to die.

—Jack London

Part I

Part I

1

It was just starting to snow when we pulled off the highway and into the parking lot of the Red Oak Tavern.

There was nothing special to the place, a couple of gas pumps out front and a neon open sign buzzing its welcome behind dirty glass. The inside was clean and warm and smelled like grease and onions, and by the time the waitress brought our coffee, I'd managed to shake the road out of my head and was beginning to feel alive again.

We sat for a while, not saying much, drinking our coffee. We were the only ones inside except for a man whispering into a pay phone on the other side of the lunch counter. I don't think we would've noticed him at all if it wasn't for his cough. The sound, wet and choking, was hard to ignore.

I did my best.

Sara didn't.

"My grandfather had a cough like that," she said. "Right before he died. It was terrible."

"It doesn't sound good."

"When he got real bad, he'd cough and spray blood and mucus all over everything, his clothes, the furniture, the walls, everything." She sipped her coffee. "Do you know what it's like having to pick scabs out of your hair at night because someone coughed blood on you?"

I told her I didn't.

"It's not fun, believe me."

"Probably worse for him."

Sara looked at me then nodded. "Yeah, you're right. It was terrible for him." She reached for the sugar and opened three packets into her coffee then tossed the empties on the growing stack in the ashtray. "People understood and I don't think anyone blamed him in the end, considering how much pain he was in and all."

"Blamed him?"

"For killing himself." She took another sip of the coffee and frowned. "You know, they say decaf tastes the same, but it doesn't. I can tell the difference."

"You never told me about that."

"About what?"

"Your grandfather killing himself."

"The cancer would've got him anyway," she said. "He knew the longer he stuck around the more the insurance companies would've tried to screw him. I might've done the same thing if I was him."

"Not me."

"You're not in that situation, so you don't know."

I started to argue then felt a dull wave of pain build behind my eyes. I looked down and pressed my fingers against the sides of my head.

"You okay?" Sara asked.

I told her I was.

"Your head?"

I nodded.

"Do you have your pills?"

"Took them already," I said. "It'll pass."

"I can drive some, if you want."

"I'll be fine. Finish your story."

"Not much to finish," Sara said. "It is what it is."

I sat back, and neither of us spoke for a long time.

The only other sound in the room was Hank Williams, far away and lonely, singing "Lovesick Blues" through hidden speakers in the ceiling. I wasn't a big fan of country music, but there was something about Hank Williams that always put me in a good mood.

Shame how he died.

A few minutes later, the man at the pay phone slammed the receiver down then walked to the lunch counter and sat on one of the stools. He coughed, then lifted a glass of water and drank. It didn't help, and he coughed again.

Each time he did, Sara winced.

"That poor man," she said. "He sounds awful."

I didn't say anything.

Behind me, the kitchen doors opened and our waitress came out carrying two plates stacked with food.

Sara smiled. "It's about time."

The waitress crossed the dining room and set the plates in front of us. She asked if we needed anything else. I told her we didn't, and she set a half-empty bottle of ketchup on the table then disappeared back into the kitchen.

I stared at my burger for a moment then closed my eyes. The pain in my head was fading, but the pills were making my stomach spin. I wasn't sure if I'd be able to eat, so I wanted to take my time.

Sara didn't wait. She pushed her dark hair behind her ears and reached for her burger. By the time I took my first bite, she was almost finished.

"Damn, I was starved," she said.

I agreed, and neither of us said much as we ate.

Eventually, my stomach settled, and when I started to slow down I set what was left of my burger on the plate and said, "So, how did he do it?"

The man at the counter wheezed and coughed.

"How'd who do what?"

"Your grandfather," I said. "How'd he kill himself?"

Sara frowned. "That's a little morbid."

"You don't have to tell me."

"I don't mind. I'm just teasing you." She licked the grease off her index finger and pointed it at the center of her chest and said, "Shotgun, right here. Big mess."

"You're kidding."

She shook her head then picked up a bundle of fries and ran them through a pool of salted ketchup on her plate and took a bite. "My daddy said he killed himself like a man, whatever that means. My grandma said it was because he wanted an open casket at his funeral. She said if he had a weakness, it was vanity."

"Do you miss him?"

"Not really," she said. "I was young, and the only memory I have is being outside with him in his tomato garden. Those vines were so tall, they seemed to go up and up forever." She looked down at her plate then picked up a few more fries. "That's a good memory, I guess."

I didn't say anything else. Instead, I sat and watched her eat and tried to imagine her as a young girl standing in her grandfather's tomato garden, safe and happy under a vaulted blue Minnesota sky.

Sara must've seen something in my eyes because she smiled then leaned across the table and kissed me long and soft.

Her lips tasted like fryer oil and salt.

"It's okay, baby," she said. "We all bounce till we break."

———

Something shattered behind me and I turned.

The man at the counter was fumbling with the napkin dispenser and fighting to breathe. There was broken glass on the floor and water ran off the edge of the counter in thin streams.

The waitress came over with a dish towel and started picking up the broken glass. The man tried to speak, but every few words were broken by another long hacking string of coughs.

"You think he's okay?" Sara asked.

I didn't answer.

I watched him get up and reach for a green backpack on the stool next to him. He slid the strap over his shoulder then weaved his way through the empty tables toward the bathrooms in the back of the diner. He held a crumpled stack of napkins over his mouth as he walked.

"He needs a doctor," Sara said.

"Looks that way."

"You should go see if he's okay."

I ignored her and watched him until the men's room door closed, then I picked up my burger and finished the last few bites. I could still hear the man coughing, but it was muffled and far away.

A few minutes later, the waitress came by and refilled our coffee.

Sara thanked her then said, "Is that guy okay?"

"Doesn't sound like it," the waitress said. "I'm just hoping he doesn't die back there. I need to make it home to my kids before this storm hits."

I looked out the window at the parking lot and saw our car, already covered with a thin layer of snow. The sky around it swirled thick and gray.

"How bad is it supposed to get?"

"How far you going?"

"Reno."

The waitress clicked her tongue and said, "You might still get ahead of it if you hurry, but if I were you, I'd double back and head over to I-80."

"Into the storm?" Sara shook her head. "This way is quicker."

"Not if they close the road, it ain't." The waitress nodded toward the window. "The plows don't make it back here until I-80 is clear. If this storm is as bad as they say, and they end up closing the highway, you might be out here for a while."

Sara looked at me. Her eyes shone green under the plastic glare of the fluorescent lights. "What do you think?"

"What's the quickest way to I-80?"

"About fifteen miles back," the waitress said. "Maybe twenty."

"That's a long way," Sara said. "It seems kinda crazy to turn around now, don't you think?"

"Up to you guys," the waitress said. "Who knows, you might be able to stay ahead of it. Maybe it's not as bad as people are saying."

Sara looked at me and shrugged.

I thanked the waitress then she took our plates and pushed the check across the table toward me. When she was gone, I looked out the window at the snow and the low rolling sky.

"I don't want to go back to I-80, Nate. Do you?"

I shook my head. "It doesn't look all that bad right now. I bet we can stay ahead of it."

"Good."

The man in the bathroom coughed again, harder this time, and I saw Sara tense across from me. She looked up and I knew what was coming.

"It's not our business," I said.

"He's all alone out here, and he sounds really sick."

"He's a grown-up. He knows what's best for him."

"Please, Nate? Just go check on him."

The last thing I wanted to do was talk to a complete stranger in the men's bathroom at a roadside diner. I tried to explain this to her, but she didn't get it. Instead, she looked at me in a way she had of looking at me, and I knew there was no point in arguing.

Besides, I'd had a few cups of coffee and we had a long drive ahead. I was going back there anyway.

I didn't see how I could say no.

2

I was pissing on either Cat Stevens or Osama bin Laden, it was hard to tell. The photo on the urinal filter was old and faded and all I could see was the beard.

I decided it really didn't matter.

The man from the lunch counter was shuffling around in one of the stalls. He wasn't coughing like before, but I could hear him breathing. Obviously, he wasn't dead, so I didn't see the point in checking.

I zipped up and walked over to the sink. The light above the mirror was sharp and white and turned my reflection a cold gray. I stared into the glass and examined the dark circles under my eyes, then I reached for the faucet and stopped.

There was blood in the sink, and it was fresh.

I glanced back at the stall then grabbed a paper towel from a stack on the counter and used it to turn on the faucet. The soap dispenser was empty, so I ran my hands under the water for a long time. When I finished, I used another paper towel to shut the faucet off.

The man in the stall coughed.

I looked down at the blood, almost black under the cold white light, and thought about Sara's grandfather.

I wanted to leave.

I took a fresh paper towel and dried my hands then opened the door leading back into the diner. All I had to do was walk out, but something wouldn't let me go.

I stood there for a long time, trying to decide.

Eventually, I let the door close, then I walked back to the stall and knocked.

The movement inside stopped.

I waited for the man to say something. When he didn't, I said, "None of my business, but I wanted to see if you were okay. That cough sounds pretty bad."

Silence.

I stood, listening to the echo of the pipes behind the tile walls, then stepped away. I was about to leave when I heard the latch slide and saw the stall door inch open.

The man's face appeared, colorless and coated with sweat. He looked from me to the door then back.

"What did you say?"

I started to explain about Sara and how she'd asked me to check on him, but his eyes kept moving from me to the door, and I could tell he wasn't listening. Eventually, he turned and grabbed his backpack and slipped it over his shoulder then pushed past me toward the sink.

The man wasn't tall, but his shoulders were wide and strong. He had a thick pink scar that started on his neck then snaked down and disappeared under the back of his shirt.

I looked in the stall. There was blood on the toilet and the white tile floor, more than a little.

"We heard you coughing," I said. "We wanted to make sure you were—"

"Fuck."

The man slapped the empty soap dispenser with his palm, then again, this time hard enough to crack the plastic. He leaned forward on the counter and lowered his head. His shoulders sagged, and I could see them move with his breath. Eventually, he straightened and went back to rinsing his hands.

"Anyone else come in while I've been back here?"

I looked around the bathroom. I didn't know what he meant, and I stammered over my words.

"In the diner?" His voice was slow and harsh. "Has anyone else come in, sat down, ordered coffee, maybe a fucking sandwich?"

"No," I said. "No one else is out there."

The man leaned forward and splashed water on his face. When he looked up, I saw his reflection in the mirror.

Under that light, he was a corpse.

"That's good." He reached for the paper towels on the counter and ran them over his face and hands, watching me in the mirror. "What the hell happened to you?"

I didn't say anything.

The man smiled. "You look like you've been through the grinder."

I ignored him. "So, you going to be okay?"

The man shook his head, then laughed under his breath. "You her little errand boy?"

"What?"

"Your girl out there, the brunette." He motioned toward the dining room. "She send you back here to check up on me?"

"We just thought—"

"Man, I bet you do everything she tells you to do, don't you?" He paused. "I don't blame you. I noticed her when you two walked in. She's a tight little thing. And with the way you look, I can see why you want to keep her happy."

I held up my hands. "Just trying to be friendly, that's all."

The man crumpled the paper towels and tossed them into the trash then turned and looked at me.

I fought the urge to step back.

"Well, don't," he said. "I don't need new friends."

"My mistake."

"That's right, it was, so when you report back to your girl out there, you tell her I'm fine and then you tell her to mind her own fucking business."

He stared at me, and I did my best not to blink.

It didn't work.

The man shouldered his backpack then brushed past me, out of the men's room and into the diner.

I stood for a while, staring at the closed door, not sure what to do next. I told myself not to let it bother me, but I couldn't help it. If that was what I got for trying to be nice, then lesson learned.

Before I left, I went back to the stall and took a closer look at all the blood on the floor. I didn't know what was wrong with the guy, but it was obvious that pretty soon there was going to be one less asshole in the world.

That was good enough for me.

———

When I came out of the bathroom, the man was gone. Sara was sitting in the booth. She stared at me as I got closer, waiting.

"He's fine," I said.

"That's it?"

"What else do you want?" I picked up the check and said, "We still need gas. You ready to go?"

"Did he say anything at all?"

"Like what?"

"I don't know," she said. "Anything. He ran out of here in a hurry. You weren't nasty to him, were you?"

I looked out the window at the parking lot. There were one or two cars out there, but I didn't see him around any of them and that was just fine.

"I asked if he was okay, and he said he was."

"That's it?"

"That's it."

Sara stared at me. "You're not telling me something."

"I'm telling you what he said. Now we need to get going if we want to stay ahead of that storm, unless you want to spend the night in this diner."

Sara frowned then slid out of the booth and started back toward the bathrooms. "I'll meet you out front," she said. "But we're not through talking about this. You're hiding something from me, and I can tell. You're a shitty liar."

"I'm telling you the truth."

She didn't say anything else, just kept walking.

I stood at the table and watched her go.

Sara wasn't a beauty, at least not in a movie star sort of way, but watching her walk made me ache inside.

It was like watching something dirty.

Everything slid just right.

Once she was gone I counted out enough money to cover the bill and a small tip, then I dropped it on the table. I picked up my coffee cup and drank the last cold bit then stared out the window at the storm coming in over the empty fields lining the highway.

I thought again about turning back to I-80, but pushed the idea away. The storm was moving fast and I didn't want to take the chance of getting stuck. Our only option was to keep moving. We could still make it if we hurried.

As I was leaving, the waitress came out of the kitchen and thanked me. "You two be safe out there," she said.

I told her we'd try.

3

I watched the numbers on the gas pump roll by for a long time. It was depressing, and when I'd had enough I turned away and stared out across the parking lot toward the empty highway and the swirling snow.

The sky to the north was a black and gray mass, pulsing like something alive. It was getting closer, and I couldn't take my eyes off it. The longer I stared, the more my mind let go and twisted the clouds. Soon I was seeing shapes and faces moving behind the storm.

It wasn't a good sign.

Usually, that detached feeling was followed by blinding headaches, but since I'd already taken more of my pills than I should have, I didn't think I had anything to worry about this time.

I closed my eyes and tried my best to relax. I told myself I was just tired from the road, and that seemed to help. When I opened my eyes again, the storm was just a storm. Beautiful and cold.

"Hey, kid."

I turned around, fast.

The man from the lunch counter held up his hands and smiled. "Sorry, buddy. Didn't mean to scare you."

I told him he didn't, but my voice cracked when I spoke. I cursed myself under my breath.

He came around the car to where I was standing. He had on a thick black winter coat with a fur-lined hood, but when he spoke I could still hear the shiver in his voice.

"Sylvester White," he said. "Call me Syl."

He held out his hand.

I shook it. "Nate."

"Listen, Nate. I want to apologize for being such a prick in there. I've had a bad run of luck and I shouldn't have snapped at you. I had no right to do that."

"Don't worry about it."

"I'm not worried about it, kid. I'm trying to make it right. I don't like acting that way. It makes me look like an asshole."

I didn't argue.

Syl crossed his arms over his chest and said, "It's fucking freezing out here."

Being from Minnesota, I didn't think it was too bad, but I kept that to myself. Instead, I motioned toward the storm and said, "Looks like it's gonna get worse."

Syl looked off to the north and I noticed something change in his eyes. It was like he was seeing the storm for the first time. He didn't say anything for a moment, then he turned and pointed to a white Cadillac parked on the side of the building.

"Piece of shit died on me when I pulled in," he said. "I was hoping to get to Omaha, but now it looks like I'm stuck out here until all this blows over."

"Sorry to hear it."

The gas clicked off and I replaced the nozzle on the pump and the cap on the tank then looked past Syl toward the diner.

Sara was still inside.

"Where's your girl?"

"Bathroom," I said. "Long drive."

"Where you two heading?"

"Reno."

Syl made a warm sound and smiled. "My second home. Chicago's first, but if I had my way, I'd be in the desert."

I didn't say anything.

"You got family out there?"

"Cousin." I thought about saying more, but I didn't.

A moment later, the door to the diner opened and Sara came out into the snow. She closed her coat tight around her chest then started across the parking lot toward the car.

"There she is," I said.

Syl looked then turned back to me. "Listen, kid. I know I didn't make the best first impression, and normally I'd never ask, but with the storm coming and since you're going that way, how about dropping me off in Omaha?"

I started to say no, but he stopped me.

"The airport would be great, but anywhere in the city is fine, a hotel or a bar. Someplace I can get a cab."

I shook my head. "I don't think so."

"I'd pay you, of course. Let's say three hundred dollars?"

Sara came around the passenger side and said, "What about three hundred dollars?"

Syl looked at her and smiled, big and welcoming. The change was dramatic and seamless, like it'd been rehearsed.

A warning light flashed in the back of my mind.

Syl held his hand out to Sara and introduced himself.

Sara shook it and smiled back.

"I was talking to Nate about a ride into Omaha."

He told her about his car and about the storm then repeated his offer of three hundred dollars. He finished by taking a packed money clip from the front pocket of his pants and counting three one-hundred-dollar bills off the top. It didn't make a dent in the size of the clip.

"What do you guys say?"

"I don't think so," I said.

Syl turned toward me. Behind him I saw Sara's eyes get big. She looked at me and mouthed the words "three hundred dollars."

I frowned.

"You have to do what you feel comfortable doing. I understand that, but are you sure I can't persuade you to help me out?"

"I'm afraid not," I said.

"What if we make it five hundred?" He peeled two more bills off the top. "That's a lot of money. Come on, kid, I'm desperate out here."

Sara came around the car and grabbed my hand and squeezed, hard. Her eyes never left the money. "You're not some crazy, psycho killer, are you, Syl? Tell the truth."

Syl laughed, warm and gentle, and this time when the warning light flashed, it was blinding.

"I'm afraid those days are behind me, my dear."

Sara looked up at me. "I don't see the harm, do you?"

Syl held out the bills, and even though I knew the decision had been made, I stared at them for a while before taking them.

"Thanks, kids, I appreciate it." He motioned toward the Cadillac and said, "Let me grab my suitcase and we'll get moving before that storm catches us."

Once he was gone, Sara turned and took the money from me. "Five hundred dollars." She bounced as she spoke. "Oh man, can you believe this?"

I looked past her toward Syl. He was coughing and struggling to pull a black suitcase out of the Cadillac's trunk. Eventually it came free and he started back, his face hidden in the shadows under his hood.

"I think our luck is changing." Sara fanned the bills in front of her and smiled. "And we're not even to Reno yet."

She leaned into me and raised her face to mine. A single snowflake landed on her cheek and hung, delicate and white, before dissolving against her skin.

I reached up and wiped it away with my thumb.

"Aren't you going to kiss me?" she asked.

The wind picked up. Sara didn't seem to notice.

"Are you sure you want to give him a ride?" I asked. "We don't know anything about this guy and I don't trust him. He could be—"

Sara shushed me.

"Kiss me," she said.

"I'm being serious."

"So am I," she said. "Kiss me, for good luck."

I frowned. "That doesn't work."

"Of course it does," she said. "It always works. Now kiss me."

I stared at her for a moment longer, then bent and pressed my lips against hers.

It was a good kiss.

But it didn't work.

4

Syl insisted on paying for the gas, and we didn't try to stop him. While he was inside, Sara and I waited in the car and I listened to her talk about all the things we could do with the five hundred dollars. It was nice to see her happy, but the money wouldn't last nearly as long as she thought it would. Before we knew it, we'd be right back where we started.

"You know what I'm going to do when I turn twenty-one?"

"Get drunk?"

The second the words were out of my mouth, I regretted them. I looked at Sara, but she didn't seem to care, even though on some level I knew I'd struck a nerve.

I tried to apologize, but she cut me off.

"I'm going to get a job in one of the casinos dealing blackjack," she said. "You hear those stories about big winners leaving their dealers thousand-dollar tips. Can you imagine?"

"That'd be nice," I said. "But you still have a few years to go."

"You do it then. You'd make a good dealer."

"I can't work in a casino."

"Why not? You're old enough."

"Background checks."

"They do those?"

I laughed. "With that kind of money flying around?"

"Oh." Sara was quiet for a minute, then she shrugged and said, "I guess you're right, but I'm still going to do it when the time comes."

We kept talking about what we were going to do once we got to Reno, then we saw Syl come out of the diner and cross the parking lot toward the car.

I watched him come.

Sara noticed and said, "Will you stop worrying."

I told her I'd try.

Once Syl got close, Sara got out and moved the passenger seat forward and started to climb into the back.

Syl stopped her.

"I'll take the back," he said. "This is your car."

"For five hundred dollars, I think you can ride up front."

Syl refused again, and this time Sara didn't press. I didn't blame her. Nearly everything we owned was packed into the backseat. It would've been a tight fit, even for her. Syl somehow made it work, but it wasn't easy for him.

"You gonna be okay back there?" I asked.

"Like a baby in the womb," Syl said. "Snug and warm."

Sara got in and closed the door. She turned back toward Syl. "If you change your mind, just say something. I've got short legs."

"I appreciate it, sweetheart, but I'll be fine."

Sara looked at me and shrugged.

"We ready?" I asked.

They both said we were, so I put the car in gear and pulled out of the parking lot and onto the highway.

———

At first, the roads didn't seem that bad. The snow had settled in patches along the sides, but the center was clear and we made pretty good time. All around us, thin snakes of snow slid across the asphalt then dissolved under the car as we passed.

No one said much.

I heard Syl adjust something behind me and I looked back at him in the mirror. He shifted a couple bags around then coughed and said, "You two don't travel light, do you?"

"Everything we got is back there," Sara said.

"Everything?"

"Everything worth keeping."

Syl was quiet for a moment, then he said, "Are you two running away from something or toward something?"

"What do you mean?"

Syl coughed again. "You packed everything you owned into your car then set off across the country. It seems to me you're either running away from something or toward something. I'm asking which one."

"Both, I guess," Sara said. "We're getting married."

"Is that so?"

"Just as soon as we're settled." She looked at me and smiled. "Isn't that right?"

I said it was.

"How do your parents feel about that?"

Sara laughed. "Mine aren't too happy, but they'll deal with it." She motioned toward me. "Nate's folks are dead."

"Both of them?"

"They died when I was a kid," I said. "I grew up in and out of foster homes with my little brother."

"What does he think?"

I shook my head. "He's gone, too."

"He died a few years ago in a car accident," Sara said. "Nate was driving."

I looked at her and started to say something, but my throat felt thick and I couldn't find the words. I rarely talked about what happened to my brother, and never with strangers. For her to throw it out in such a casual way stopped me cold.

I stared at her, but she was turned toward Syl and didn't notice. When she did finally look at me, she smiled and touched my arm and said, "It was tough."

"Sorry to hear it," Syl said. "What was his name?"

I cleared my throat. "Vincent."

"Is that how you got that scar? The accident?"

"No," I said. "That was something different."

"Looks like a big deal. Does it hurt?"

"Not all the time."

I think Syl was waiting for me to go on, but I didn't, and no one said anything else for a long time.

When the silence got to be too much, Sara said, "How about you, Syl. Are you married?"

"Never found the right woman. Thought I did once, but I was wrong."

"Things didn't work out?"

Syl smiled. "They sure didn't."

"That's too bad."

Syl coughed, hard, then winced.

"You okay?" Sara asked.

He nodded. "It'll pass."

"We can try to find a doctor if you'd like."

"No, thank you. I'd rather hear about your parents. What'd they say when you told them you were getting married?"

I laughed, couldn't help it.

Sara slapped my arm, then looked back at Syl. "It was a lot to take in all at once," she said. "I'm their firstborn, so it was hard for them to let go. And they're kind of religious."

"*Kind* of?" I said.

"Okay, very religious," Sara said. "They're both recovering alcoholics."

"I can see where that might be a problem."

"It's fine, whatever they want to believe, I have my own opinions."

"They didn't rub off on you?"

Sara shook her head. "I was older when they started all that stuff, so it wasn't like I grew up in church." She paused. "I never really bought into it."

"That must've upset them."

"A lot of things I've done upset them."

"Like getting married."

Sara smiled. "That's one."

"I think they were more upset about becoming grandparents than about us getting married," I said.

"You're pregnant?"

Sara looked at me and frowned. "We weren't supposed to tell anyone."

"Don't worry," Syl said. "I can keep a secret."

"It's not the reason we're getting married, you know."

"That's good."

"I didn't want to tell anyone about the baby because it's bad luck to say anything this early."

Syl made a dismissive sound. "There's no such thing as bad luck. Things either go your way or they don't." He coughed then cleared his throat. "In the end, you get what's coming to you. All that matters is how you deal with it."

"Play the cards you're dealt."

"That's right."

"Sara believes in luck."

"Some people do," Syl said. "My experience tells me different."

"What experience is that?" Sara asked. "What exactly do you do?"

"For a living?"

"Yeah," she said. "How do you make enough money to pay five hundred dollars for a ride to Omaha?"

Syl shook his head and smiled. "Truth is, I don't, but these are special circumstances." He seemed to think for a minute, then said, "I guess you can say I settle disputes for a living."

"What kind of disputes?"

"Whatever's asked of me."

"Is it boring?" Sara asked.

"Can be."

We let the subject drop and a couple minutes pass, then Sara looked back at Syl and said, "What about us running into each other out here? That was luck, wasn't it?

"Depends on how you look at it."

"I look at it like we're five hundred dollars richer, and you have a ride to Omaha."

Syl laughed. "You might have me on that one. And who knows, maybe you're right. Maybe it does all come down to luck, good and bad. I don't know for sure, one way or the other."

His voice sounded tired, and he coughed again. This time it came from deep in his chest and shook his entire body.

When he stopped, Sara said, "Syl, are you sure about not seeing a doctor?"

"Positive." He took a white handkerchief from his pocket and wiped at his mouth, then he leaned back against one of the black garbage bags we'd used to pack Sara's clothes. "I think I just need some rest. If you don't mind, I'm going to try and get some sleep."

"All right," Sara said. "But if you change your mind about the doctor—"

"I'll let you know."

Sara watched him settle in, then she turned and looked at me. I saw the concern in her eyes.

After a few minutes, I looked at Syl in the mirror and saw his eyes were closed. I thought he was asleep, but then he spoke.

"Nate, did you tell anyone about this trip?"

"What do you mean?"

"Does anyone know where you're going?"

"Not really," I said. "A few people know we're getting married, but not when or where. I figured we'd tell them afterward."

"What about your cousin in Reno?"

"We planned on surprising him."

"How about you, Sara? Your parents know you're out here?"

She shook her head. "It's our secret."

"Why do you want to know?" I asked.

Syl didn't answer, and when I looked back at him in the mirror, his eyes were closed.

———

*When I was positive he was asleep, I touched Sara's leg and mo-*tioned toward the backseat. "He's out."

She turned to look. "He must've been exhausted."

"Let's hope he sleeps the entire way. Talk about easy money."

"Don't you think he needs a doctor?"

"He says he doesn't."

Sara paused. "You don't think he has something contagious, do you?"

I hadn't thought about it until just then, and the idea stopped me for a moment. Then I decided it didn't make any difference. If he was contagious, it was too late to do anything about it now.

"I don't think so," I said. "Just don't kiss him."

Sara rolled her eyes and mouthed the word "gross."

I smiled then reached over and squeezed her leg. She put her hand on mine then leaned back and closed her eyes. Her skin was soft and warm, and after a while, she was asleep.

I drove on in silence and snowfall.

5

We'd gone almost seventy miles when it became clear we weren't going to make it to Omaha. The road was completely covered and the falling snow shattered in the headlights, making it impossible to see. I had to slow down to school zone speeds to make sure I didn't take us into one of the drainage ditches running alongside the highway.

It'd been almost twenty miles since I'd seen another car, and I felt a sense of emptiness that I couldn't shake.

We were completely alone.

At one point we passed under a single streetlight glowing yellow on the side of the road. I had no idea why it was out there in the middle of nothing. There were no houses or crossroads, just that one lonely light covered in a swarm of snow.

Occasionally, I'd see huge drifts off to the side. After the third or fourth one, it occurred to me that there could be cars buried under them, possibly with people inside.

The thought was enough to make me sit up and focus on

my driving and the road ahead. If I didn't pay attention, and we went off the road and got stuck, we could die.

Sara and Syl were both asleep. I leaned forward and turned on the radio for background noise, but we were too far out and there was no signal. I searched the dial and finally found a static-filled voice talking about the weather and the coming storm.

It was the last thing I wanted to hear.

If I needed to know how bad the storm was, all I had to do was look around. If it was worse than what I saw outside the car, I didn't want to know.

I turned the radio off.

A few more miles slid by, then I saw a sign for a motel up ahead. I thought it might be a good place to stop and wait. There was no telling what else we'd find out here, or how much farther we'd be able to go in the storm.

It was time to take what we could get.

I glanced up at Syl in the mirror, and at first I thought his eyes were open, staring at me. It was hard to tell in the dark, and I watched him until I was sure they were closed.

When I looked back, the road had curved.

I turned the wheel, sharp, and felt the back end of the car slip sideways into a snowdrift. I spun the wheel the other way and the car fishtailed from side to side, then straightened and we were back on the road.

My heart was beating heavy in my chest, and once I was sure we were safe, I did my best to calm down.

Sara opened her eyes.

"What was that?"

"What was what?"

She sat up, slow, then leaned forward and looked out at the dark sky swirling above us like smoke in a jar.

"This looks really bad."

"We're okay," I said. "Just slow moving."

I could feel my hands shake, and I squeezed the steering wheel as tight as I could to keep them steady.

In the backseat, Syl made a choking sound and I glanced up at him in the rearview. Even in the near-dark of the car, his skin shone pale and wet.

Sara turned around and said, "Syl, are you okay?"

No answer.

"I think he's still asleep," I said.

Sara stared at him then unbuckled her seat belt and climbed up on her knees and reached into the back.

"What are you doing?"

She didn't answer me.

I looked over and saw her holding her hand against his forehead.

"Don't touch him," I said.

"Nate, he's burning up."

I reached over and put my hand on her hip and tried to pull her away from him. I didn't have the leverage to do much, but Sara got the hint and let herself be pulled.

"We need to stop somewhere," she said. "He needs a doctor."

"He said he didn't want one."

"I know what he said, but I think he's really sick. I mean, really sick."

I looked back at him again.

His skin was so white it looked blue.

She was probably right.

"I saw a sign for a motel up here somewhere."

"As long as there's a phone."

We hadn't passed anything resembling civilization in over twenty miles, and I didn't have a lot of hope for the motel. If we'd been on the main interstate it would've been easy to find a phone, even a hospital. But we weren't. This road was a long, two-lane scar cut through fields and farmland. There was nothing out here but us.

Sara got up on her seat again and reached into the back and shook Syl's shoulder. "Syl?"

"What are you doing?"

"Trying to wake him up."

"Why?"

"Because I think he should be awake."

I tried to keep my eyes on the road, but I kept looking back to see if he'd wake up. He didn't, and each time he inhaled, a muddy wet wheeze sounded from somewhere deep in his chest.

I was starting to worry.

Sara shook him again, over and over, calling his name each time. Eventually his eyes opened. When they did, they were distant and unfocused, not really seeing.

He mumbled something, but I missed it.

"We're going to find you a doctor," Sara said. "Do you understand?"

"She's here, isn't she?"

"Who?"

He tried to sit up, but Sara stopped him.

"Where is she?"

"Who are you talking about?" Sara asked.

"Lilith, she's here."

Sara looked at me.

I shrugged.

She sat back in the passenger seat then turned toward me and tried to smile. "Well, at least he's awake."

I looked in the mirror and for a second, Syl's eyes cleared and he tried to sit up. It didn't work, and he struggled for breath. The sound rolled out of him like a scream, and when he spoke next, his voice was harsh and strained.

"You have my money."

"We're going to find a doctor, Syl. You'll be okay."

"No doctor."

"It's not a choice," Sara said. "You're burning up and you sound—"

"I said no fucking doctor!"

He coughed hard, and I could hear the pain underneath. When he spoke again, it was through clenched teeth.

"We have to keep going," he said. "She's following us. She knows I'm out here."

"Who?"

"The whore."

I could tell he was fading again, so I said, "Who's following us?"

Syl ignored me. "You can't have it. I won't let you take it."

"Take what?" I asked. "What are you talking about?"

Syl closed his eyes, didn't answer.

I looked at Sara. "What the hell is he talking about?"

"No idea," she said. "He's delirious."

I stopped looking back and focused on the road. I could still hear him breathing and mumbling about liars and money.

Every now and then he'd raise his voice and accuse us of being thieves.

I wanted to tell him that he could have his money back, and he could walk the rest of the way to Omaha, for all I cared, but of course I didn't.

As far as I was concerned, we'd earned that money.

Every cent of it.

————

Sara tried to keep Syl awake, but after a while she gave up and sat back in her seat. "We have to pull over somewhere, Nate."

"I know it."

"We need a phone."

"I know it," I said. "That motel is supposed to be up here somewhere."

I noticed she was shaking and I put my hand on her leg and squeezed. "It's okay."

"Jesus, Nate, what if he dies back there?"

"He's not going to die."

I wanted to keep her mind off Syl, so I reached between the seats for the road atlas then held it out to her. "See if you can tell where we are. Maybe there's something listed."

She took the atlas and turned on the overhead light. The glare made it hard to see the road, and I leaned forward against the steering wheel.

"Did we pass Norrisville?"

I told her we had, a long time ago.

She read off a few other towns, and eventually we figured out where we were.

It wasn't good.

We had another thirty miles to the next major turnoff and another twenty from there to the interstate. At the speed we were going, it would take hours.

I hoped the sign for the motel had been right.

"Oh my God, Nate."

"There's nothing we can do," I said. "Let's just let him sleep."

Sara looked back at him for a long time, then turned and stared at the road ahead and didn't say a word.

The highway was nearly invisible behind the snow, and I was beginning to think the sign for the motel was wrong, or that we'd passed it in the storm, when I saw headlights flash along the side of the road.

Sara saw them, too, and she sat up fast.

"What's that?"

I wasn't sure.

The headlights flashed again, then we saw a car turn and disappear behind what looked like a small house. When we got closer, I saw several small buildings, all wood, and all spread out around a parking lot. It looked like a motel, but there were no lights in any of the windows and the neon sign out front was black.

I felt my stomach sink.

"I think it's closed."

"There was a car," Sara said. "Someone's there."

I slowed down and felt the tires spin against the snow, then I turned into the parking lot.

I could see the outline of a palm tree above the motel's sign. The neon letters under the tree were blacked out but big enough so that I could still read them in the dark: THE OASIS INN.

There was a main office behind the sign, and I pulled in and stopped across from the front door. A line of buildings stretched out in two directions from the main parking lot. Beyond them, just past the range of my headlights, I saw the storm-faded shapes of playground swings and slides.

"Are they open?" Sara asked.

I told her I didn't know.

No lights were on, but there was a soft amber glow coming through the windows. Someone was inside.

"I'm going to knock," I said.

Sara looked back at Syl. "Just hurry, okay?"

When I got out of the car, the wind hit hard and sucked the air out of me. I kept my head down and kicked through the snow toward the front door.

There was a covered walkway out front that ran the length of the building. Once I got under it, I looked back and saw Sara leaning over her seat and holding her hand against Syl's forehead.

I didn't like to see her touching him.

Contagious or not, I wanted him out of my car as soon as possible. It wasn't the kindest attitude, but right then, I didn't care.

What Syl needed was a hospital.

Once we found one, he'd be someone else's problem. Maybe they could track down Lilith, whoever she was, and get her to come and take him home.

Either way, it wouldn't be my problem.

The five hundred dollars he paid us was great, but there were limits to what I'd do for money.

6

I tried the door, and when it didn't open I leaned against the glass and looked inside. There were several candles set up along the front desk and in the corners of the office. They were lit and they filled the room with a soft gold light.

I could see an open door along the far wall, and beyond it, the jagged reflection of a fire burning in a fireplace.

I tried the door again then knocked on the glass.

A moment later a shadow moved in the back room and a man came out into the office. He waved to me then came over and turned the lock.

I stepped back and let the door swing open. When it did, a set of welcome bells chimed above me.

The man in the office was small but built thick. At first I thought he was just a kid, then, when my eyes adjusted to the light, I saw the deep lines on his face and the aged green tattoos on his forearms.

He definitely wasn't a kid.

"Sorry about that," the man said. "We make it a habit of

locking up after dark. We've got a late-night buzzer, but the damned thing ain't working tonight."

He stepped away from the door and I went in. The room felt as warm as it'd looked from outside.

"You get turned around, too?"

"What?"

"Highway's closed up by Ridgemont." He walked around the front desk. "State patrol's not letting anyone through tonight."

"I didn't see any cars out there."

"We've had one or two, but most people aren't crazy enough to be out in this storm, especially on this road." He waved me off. "No matter. Tonight's a bad night for guests anyway. It's probably for the best."

"You got a phone?"

"Sure, but it's down. Phone's out, power's out, nothing's working. We've got gas heat, thank God, otherwise—"

"No phone?"

"No nothing," he said. "We got running water and warm rooms and that's about it. I was back in the kitchen moving food into coolers so it doesn't go bad, just in case we're stuck like this for a while."

"Any idea how long?"

He pointed to an old dial radio on a shelf behind the desk. "I got this thing running on batteries, but all it tells me is there's more snow coming, like I needed to be told."

"How about a doctor? Is there one around?"

"Not close."

"A hospital?"

The expression on the man's face told me the answer.

"There's no hospital around here," he said. "There's a clinic about forty miles north in Frieberg, but you're not going to get there tonight, not in this storm."

I felt the frustration build in my chest and I could feel myself slipping. I did my best to stay calm, but when I spoke again there was an edge to my voice.

"If there's no doctor, what do you people do if someone breaks an arm or a leg, then what?"

"Well, that's never happened that I can recall," he said. "But if it did, I suppose we'd have to get someone to give us a ride to the clinic in Frieberg, but we can't really do that tonight, can we?" He spoke slowly, like he was talking to a small child. "You have been outside, right? You've seen the snow?"

I turned away and walked back to the door and stared at my face reflecting gold in the black window. I forced myself to calm down, then I went over my options.

There weren't many.

"You got someone sick out there?"

I told him I did, and that it might be something serious.

The man nodded. "I feel for you, but all we've got here is a warm place to rest." He paused. "There's a chance the phones might be back up tomorrow. If they are, we can call for an ambulance."

"Sounds like my only choice."

"Yes, it does." He reached behind the counter and took out a blue notebook and a pen. "No way to get into the computer until the power's back, so you'll have to pay for the room later. I'll take down some of your information now, if you don't mind."

I took the driver's license out of my wallet and set it on the counter.

"Minnesota, eh?"

It was the worst attempt at a northern accent I'd ever heard, and I couldn't bring myself to smile, not even to be polite.

I stood and watched him copy my name and address into the notebook. While he did, I tried to decipher the tattoos on his arm.

The ink was swamp water green and most of the detail was gone. The only one I could make out was a dark-haired woman bent over an anchor with one hand against her cheek in a classic pinup pose. The others were harder. One might've been an eagle with a flowing banner in its claws. The words on the banner were lost to time.

When the man finished, he handed everything back and said, "A lot of times, a good night's sleep is all someone needs. Maybe your friend will feel better in the morning."

"You might be right."

"I usually am."

I motioned toward the radio on the shelf. "What's the latest on the storm? Any good news?"

"They say it'll clear up tomorrow, but you can't trust 'em. I saw a girl on the TV last night telling me we'd only get a few inches." He pointed outside with the end of his pen. "Got to be at least six out there now, and it just keeps coming down."

"Closer to eight, I'd say."

The man shook his head. "I wouldn't be surprised if that doubles before it's done. These spring blizzards can get nasty." He turned and opened a scarred wooden cabinet behind the desk. Inside was a pegboard lined with keys. He took one out and set it on the counter next to the notebook. "I'll put you in building three, just around the corner. If you need anything, let me know."

I looked at the key and smiled.

Number thirteen.

"There are glass ashtrays in the room." He took a box of milk white emergency candles from the shelf. "I'd appreciate it if you burned these in them and not on the furniture. And make sure you keep the flame away from the curtains or anything else that can catch fire."

"I'll be careful."

"You need matches?"

I told him I didn't, but he ignored me and fished a half-empty matchbook out of his breast pocket and held it out. There was a rainbow on the cover. On the back, in neon pink and green letters, were the words THE MAXX along with a phone number.

"Those should get you through the night. And like I said, let me know if you need anything else or if your friend gets worse. Just knock and I'll hear you. I'm usually up all night anyway."

I thanked him then started toward the door. Halfway there I stopped and turned back. "What was your name?"

"Butch Sollars," he said. "U.S. Navy, retired."

He held out his hand and I shook it.

"Real name is Emerson, but I go by Butch. Nobody's called me Emerson since my mother, and I didn't like it much then, either."

"I'll remember," I said. "And thanks again."

Butch nodded. "You stay warm out there."

I pulled my coat tight then walked out into the cold. I thought about what Sara was going to say when I showed her the room number and told her the news about the phones.

All I knew was that she wasn't going to be happy.

7

I walked out of the office with my head down, shielding my face from the wind. The footprints I'd made on my way in were already half filled with fresh snow, and for the first time, the idea that we might actually be stuck seemed more like a reality than ever.

I stepped off the walkway toward the car, then I heard Sara's voice behind me.

"Nate?"

She was crouched against the building in the dark. Her legs were tucked into her chest and she had her arms wrapped around her knees. She was shaking, but when I knelt next to her and put my hand against her cheek, her skin felt warm.

"What are you doing? It's freezing."

"I think he's dead."

I felt the cold air catch in the back of my throat, and I turned toward the car. The snow had covered the windshield and I couldn't see inside.

"He's not dead."

"He's not breathing."

"He's sick, that's all."

"I don't think so. I think he's dead."

"Sara, come on."

"Go check."

I didn't move right away, and Sara stared at me, silent, then she put her head against her knees and started rocking back and forth against the building.

I got up and walked to the passenger side and opened the door. The overhead light came on, yellow and bright, and turned all the windows to black mirrors. I slid the passenger seat forward then angled down to look inside.

Syl was in the same position he'd been in when I went into the office, but the deep, wheezing rasp was gone. Sara was right, it didn't look like he was breathing.

I watched him for any signs of movement, then I leaned in and pressed my fingers against his neck. I didn't feel a pulse, but I wasn't sure I was doing it right, either. I'd only seen it done in movies.

"Is he dead?"

"I don't think he's breathing."

Sara pushed herself up and came closer. She stopped at the edge of the walkway and said, "I knew it. I knew he was dead." Her voice shook. "God, Nate, what are we going to do?"

"I don't know."

"Are you sure he's dead?"

I held my fingers against his neck for a while longer then said, "I can't find a pulse, but I'm not sure."

"Check his wrist, that's easier."

Syl's right arm was tucked against his side, and I lifted it up and pressed my fingers against his wrist. When I did, I felt something wet on his skin. I pulled my hand away and held my fingers up to the overhead light.

Sara was watching over my shoulder, and when she saw my hand she said, "Is that blood?"

I didn't say anything. Instead, I reached down and opened Syl's jacket. The right side of his shirt was wet and coated red, and I could see a tattered white bandage showing above his beltline.

"Is that blood?"

I pictured the diner and the blood on the bathroom floor, how it'd looked black under that pale white light.

"Answer me, Nate."

"Yeah," I said. "It's blood."

"From what?" I could hear the panic building in her voice. "What happened to him?"

"I don't know," I said. "But there's a lot of it."

Sara said something else, but it got lost in the wind, and I let it go.

I looked around and found an old McDonald's bag on the floor behind my seat. I picked it up and took out a few crumpled napkins and used them to lift the edge of Syl's shirt. The bandage was taped to his side and soaked through. I used one of the napkins to lift one corner, and when I did, the skin underneath tore and the wound seeped thick and black.

The smell was horrible.

I looked away for a moment, then lifted the bandage farther. The wound was small and round and the flesh surrounding it was bruised purple. I leaned closer, and once again the smell made me pull away.

The burger I'd eaten earlier climbed to the back of my throat, and I had to swallow hard to keep it there. For a second, I thought it wasn't going to stay down and I backed out of the car, fast, and spit into the snow.

"Jesus."

When I looked up, Sara was gone.

I turned and saw her moving through the snow toward the office. I ran after her, and when I got close I reached for her arm.

"Wait."

She pulled away. There were tears on her face.

"I'm going to call the cops," she said. "We have to tell them."

"We can't. The phones are out."

She didn't look like she understood, so I went over everything Butch told me. When I finished, I took the matches and the emergency candles from my pocket and handed them to her.

"There's heat in the rooms," I said. "But that's it."

Sara stared at the candles before taking them. "Did he know how long the phones would be down?"

I told her he didn't have any idea. "It depends on how long this snow keeps coming."

I thought she was going to say something else. Instead, she squeezed her arms to her chest and looked back at the car.

I asked if she was okay.

She didn't answer. "Do we just leave him out here?"

"Probably the best place. It's cold."

"What do you think happened to him?"

"I don't know for sure, but he's got a hole in his side, right about—"

"A hole? You think someone shot him?"

I nodded and pointed to a spot just under my rib cage. "Looks like it to me."

Her eyes went wide. "Are you sure?"

"How the hell can I be sure? I'm just telling you what it looks like, that's all."

That was a lie. I'd seen gunshot wounds before. I knew exactly what they looked like.

We both stood for a while, silent, letting the snow build up around us. I noticed she was shivering and I stepped in and wrapped my arms around her shoulders. This time her skin felt cold.

"You need to get inside."

She didn't argue.

I held out the key and the box of candles and told her about burning them in the ashtrays.

"Building number three," I said. "I'm going to go back and tell Butch what's going on, then I'll pull the car around and bring in the bags."

Sara nodded and took the key. She stared at it for a moment then turned it over in her hands. When she saw the room number, she didn't say a word.

It was like she'd expected it.

8

I waited until Sara was gone, then I went back to the office and knocked on the door. There was no answer and no movement behind the glass. I knocked again.

Still nothing.

I went back to the car and took an old blanket from one of the bags in the trunk, then I climbed in the passenger side and used it to cover Syl's body. I'm not sure why, it just felt like the right thing to do.

When I finished, no part of him was showing.

As I got out of the car, I noticed Syl's green backpack on the seat next to him. I grabbed it and slung it over my shoulder then closed the door and walked around to the driver's side and got in. The car was still running. I turned on the wipers to push away the snow.

I ran through what I was going to tell Butch, and eventually the police. The more I thought about it, the more I felt a sick sense of dread form in my chest. I hadn't done anything wrong, but that didn't matter. Dealing with the cops made me nervous, even when there wasn't a dead body involved.

Once they ran my name through their computer, there would be questions. They'd probably call back to Minnesota to make sure I was allowed out of the state. I wasn't too worried about that, my probation was over. I could go wherever I wanted. Still, there was always a chance someone might make a mistake.

It was a stupid thought, but one I couldn't shake.

I told myself that I'd done my time and I was a free man, but the idea of dealing with the police made my heart race. Prison will do that to you, especially if you never wanted to go back.

I sat for a while longer, letting my mind play out all the different options. I couldn't keep them straight and soon I started to feel something cold and sharp build behind my eyes.

I needed to calm down so I pressed my fingertips against the sides of my head and ran backward through the alphabet.

"Z, Y, X, W, V, U . . ."

It was a trick I'd picked up in the hospital from one of the orderlies. He was an old guy and an alcoholic, and I think he felt sorry for me. He told me it helped him focus when he was alone and bleeding for a drink.

I tried it, and it'd worked.

I'd used it ever since.

Once I felt things return to normal, I looked down at the backpack then turned it over and unzipped the main compartment. At first all I saw were clothes.

Dress shirts and black socks, all folded perfectly.

I pushed them aside.

Underneath was a clear plastic bag. I took it out and held it up to the overhead light. There were alcohol wipes inside, along with a sewing kit, a package of sterile gauze, and a roll of cloth tape.

I put it back and dug deeper.

When my hand touched something metal, I wasn't surprised. I knew exactly what I'd found.

The gun was small, a twenty-two caliber with a twelve-round magazine. There was nothing out of the ordinary about it, except for the dull gray suppressor tube attached to the barrel.

That stopped me.

Before I went to jail, guns had been my business.

I'd sold more weapons out of the trunk of my car than most legit dealers, and I made pretty good money at it, too. Not enough to retire on, but enough to get Vincent away from foster care.

Now those days were gone, but I still knew about guns and the people who bought them, and I could think of only one reason someone would mount a silencer on a twenty-two.

I held the gun in front of me and checked the safety, then I slid the clip out and counted the bullets.

Two were missing.

"Fuck."

I pushed the clip back in, then set the gun on the passenger seat. I stared at it for a while then searched the rest of the backpack.

There was nothing else inside, so I turned the bag over and checked the side pockets.

Inside, I found two stacks of one-hundred-dollar bills.

The first had a paper band wrapped tight around the center of the stack. The amount printed on the band was $10,000. The second stack was unwrapped and smaller, but not by much.

I ran my fingers back and forth over the bills.

It was mesmerizing.

I sat there and tried to figure out what to do next.

The more I thought about it, the less I wanted to talk to Butch. At least not right away.

Eventually, I put the car in gear and eased my way through the snow to building number three.

All I needed was some time to think.

———

I knocked on number thirteen and waited.

Sara opened the door then turned and crawled into bed with her back to me. Two of the candles were burning in ashtrays on the nightstand. As I stepped inside, the flames flickered but they didn't go out.

"I'm going to get the bags."

Sara didn't say anything.

It took a couple trips to get them all. Once they were inside, I sat at the small table next to the window and kicked the snow off my boots.

Sara rolled over and watched me.

"Who do you think shot him?"

"Why are you thinking about that?"

"I can't help it. He seemed like such a nice man."

"He wasn't," I said. "He was an asshole and a good actor."

"That's a thing to say." She watched me. "You promised me

you were going to work on being a better person. Are you over that now?"

"I'm working on it."

"Good, because it's important to me, Nate. No more bad energy. Not anymore."

"I know." I tried to change the subject. "Why don't you tell me who you think shot him? What's your theory?"

She watched me for a moment longer then turned away and said, "What bothers me is why he didn't want to go to a doctor. He must've known how bad he was hurt."

"Maybe he couldn't risk it. Maybe the police were after him."

"I doubt that."

"You never know about people and their secrets," I said. "We didn't know the guy. He could've been anyone."

"I like to think I'm a good judge of character. I can tell if—" She looked at me and frowned. "What's wrong with you?"

"What do you mean?"

"What's so damn funny?"

"Not a thing."

"Then why are you smiling?"

"I didn't realize I was."

"Well, you were, and I wish you'd stop. That man is dead out there, Nate. Murdered." She paused. "Do you really think that's funny?"

"Of course not."

"What did the guy in the office say when you told him?"

"I didn't tell him."

"Why not?"

"He wasn't there."

"Then go back later and tell him."

I started to explain then I stopped and tossed Syl's backpack on the bed at Sara's feet.

"What's this?"

"His backpack."

Sara shook her head. "I don't want it. Leave it in the car."

"Look inside."

She refused, so I leaned over and unzipped the bag and took out the twenty-two and set it on the bed. When she saw it, she sat up fast, pushing herself back and into the headboard.

I couldn't help but laugh.

"It's not a snake," I said. "It won't kill you."

"My God, Nate, is that his?"

I told her it was then pointed out the silencer and the two missing bullets. "Small, easy to hide, and with the suppressor, you'd barely hear it at all."

"Get rid of it."

"What for?"

"Are you kidding me? You know what'll happen if you get caught with a gun."

"I won't get caught."

She started to say something else, then I picked up the twenty-two and turned it over in my hands.

She stopped talking.

"I wish you'd put it away," she said.

"Makes you wonder what Syl was up to, doesn't it?"

"What do you mean?"

"This is an assassin's weapon," I said. "Small, silent, powerful enough to kill. All you got to do is get someone in the eye or the temple and they're done, and without the mess you'd get with the bigger—"

"You think he was a killer?"

"He did say he settled disputes for a living."

"That doesn't mean he was a killer."

"Then what about everything else? What about this gun and him being shot? It all fits."

"There are other explanations."

"Yeah, like what?"

"Self-defense."

"You don't want a silencer for self-defense. You want it to be noisy. You want to scare people off and attract attention."

Sara looked away and didn't say anything.

"There's more."

"I don't want to hear anymore."

I flipped the backpack over and took the two stacks of money out of the side pocket. I held them up in the candlelight then tossed them on the bed. Several bills came loose and slid across the sheets.

"Who do you know that carries twenty grand around in a backpack?"

Sara looked at the money for a moment, then she reached down and picked up a few of the bills, then a few more. She didn't speak.

"There's some missing out of that one," I said. "But I bet we'll find it in that money clip he's carrying."

"This is his?" Sara asked, her voice soft. "All of it?"

"Used to be," I said. "Now I'd say it's ours."

"No." She let the word hang, then she set the money on the bed and started restacking the bills. "We can't keep this, Nate. It's stealing."

"I don't think he's going to miss it, do you?"

"It's not ours."

"It's as much ours as anyone else's, maybe more. Look at what we've had to deal with tonight."

"You think the police will agree with you?"

"The police aren't going to find out. This is our secret."

"We have to tell them the truth."

"We will," I said. "We'll tell them he asked for a ride and died in the car. We'll tell them we stopped here to find a doctor, but the phones were out and the highway was closed and sorry, but that's just the way things go sometimes. End of story." I held up one finger. "And, it's the truth."

"What about the money?"

"That's between you and me."

Sara stared at the bills for a long time. "I don't know, Nate. It's a lot of money to just keep."

"It's a lot of money to just give away, too."

"Okay, but—"

She looked at me, and I could tell she wanted to be convinced, so I moved to the bed and grabbed her and kissed her, hard.

"Nate, stop."

"Don't you see what we've got here?"

She didn't say anything.

"You're the one who always talks about karma and good luck. Well, this is great fucking luck." I picked up the money and held it in front of her. "Think about what we can do with twenty thousand dollars. Think about what we can do for the baby."

That got her attention.

When she looked up, there were tears in her eyes. "For the baby?"

"Yeah," I said. "For the baby."

9

We talked for a while longer, and eventually Sara began to open up to the idea of keeping the money. She still wasn't as excited about it as I was, but I knew that would come. All she needed was time.

"I'm going to take a shower," she said.

"How are you feeling?"

"I'm okay. Tired. Worried."

"Nothing to be worried about."

She nodded then got up and grabbed one of the candles off the nightstand and walked back to the bathroom. I watched her set the candle on the sink then look at herself in the mirror.

She stood like that for a moment, then she turned and leaned into the doorway and said, "Do you think we could buy a house?"

"With twenty thousand dollars?" I smiled. "No."

"But we could put a down payment on one, couldn't we?"

"I suppose we could."

Sara stared past me at nothing. "I've never lived in an actual house before."

"Me neither."

We were both quiet for a while, then she backed into the bathroom and said, "I'll be out in a few."

I watched the door close then I reached for my jacket and took a cigarette out of the inside pocket and lit it off the candle burning on the nightstand.

"Nate, not inside."

I sighed, then stood up and said, "I'm going."

Sara had made me promise to quit smoking once the baby came, but that wasn't for a while. Until then, I smoked outside. At first I complained, but then she started reading me articles on what cigarette smoke does to kids, even before they're born. None of it was good, and since it was so important to her, I went along with it.

I slid my coat on then opened the door and stepped outside into the cold. The building blocked most of the wind, but the snow was still coming down hard.

I stood under the walkway and watched.

The cigarette was my first since that afternoon, and it went fast. When it got down to the filter, I took another one from my pocket and lit it off the first, then I walked down to the edge of our building and looked around the parking lot.

There were a few cars scattered around, but not many. Some looked old, like they hadn't moved in years, but it was hard to tell what was under all the snow. One thing for sure, the motel was far from full.

From where I was, I could see the playground at the far end

of the parking lot. It was too dark to see clearly, but I was able to pick out swings and monkey bars and several small animal rides mounted on springs. All of it was set up in a circle around what looked like a giant turtle.

I didn't think I was seeing it right.

A giant turtle didn't seem to fit, and I thought about walking out there for a closer look. I'd almost convinced myself that it wasn't that far when I heard a door slam shut on the other side of the building.

I walked around and saw a large metal shed directly behind our room. There were no windows and the sides were rusted and old. The door was standing open, wavering in the wind.

A moment later, a man came out into the snow.

He had on a brown Carhart jacket and a black knitted cap and he was carrying an industrial flashlight and a brown paper bag. Once outside, he turned and pushed the door closed then started walking through the snow toward the parking lot.

I stepped back into the darkness and didn't say anything. Once he was gone, I came around and watched him cross the parking lot and go into the building across from ours. I wasn't sure why I didn't want him to see me, it just seemed like the smart thing to do.

I felt dumb for being so jumpy, but it'd been a strange day so I figured I had an excuse.

I stayed outside until I finished my cigarette, then I dropped it in the snow and started back to the room. I'd made it halfway when I heard the shed door creak open then slam shut. A moment later, it creaked open again.

I walked back to look.

This time there was no one at the shed, but the door was standing open. Occasionally, a gust of wind would come up and the door would slam shut before drifting open again.

I stepped off the walkway and crossed through the snow. My plan was to close the door, but when I got to the shed and tried to slide the bolt, I saw that it was frozen and wouldn't move.

I stepped back and looked around for something heavy to force the bolt. Everything was covered with snow, so I opened the door and went inside. It took a minute for my eyes to adjust to the darkness. Once they did, I started looking around for something I could use.

The air in the shed was cold and had the poison sweet smell of ammonia and bleach. There wasn't much inside except a workbench at one end and a line of empty pig pens along the other. I started toward the workbench then stopped halfway.

In the dark, I could just make out the outline of several plastic buckets and glass milk jugs on the bench. There were several burners set up, along with rubber tubes that snaked up toward a duct-taped hole cut into the side of the shed wall. Next to the workbench, stacked along the side, were several empty bottles of cleaning products and a canvas bag filled with rocket-sized fireworks.

I knew what I'd found, and it was time to go.

I backed out of the shed and closed the door. It wouldn't stay shut, but I didn't care. The last thing I wanted was to be caught snooping around someone's meth lab.

I crossed through the snow with my heart throbbing inside my chest. It all made sense. The motel was in the middle of nowhere, deserted. It was the perfect place for a meth lab.

Why not?

I decided I wasn't going to tell Sara.

She didn't need the extra stress.

When I got back to our building, I walked around to the front. My eyes kept drifting toward the room across from ours.

I wasn't sure, but I thought I could see someone standing in the window. There was a shadow, but I told myself it was only a reflection of the storm in the glass.

Then the shadow moved.

It was gone.

10

Sara was still in the shower when I went inside. I took off my jacket and my boots then pushed the curtains away from the window and looked out at the building across the parking lot. I didn't see anyone, and eventually I let the curtain drop.

I crossed the room and sat on the edge of the bed and listened to the sound of running water coming from the bathroom. After a while, I leaned back on the pillows and stared up at the ceiling and the thin shadows twitching in the candlelight. I let my thoughts wander, but they kept coming back to that shed out back.

I could feel a dull ache growing in the center of my head. I tried to clear my mind and think about something else, but nothing seemed to work. Eventually, I sat up and grabbed the backpack off the floor and dumped it out on the bed.

I picked up the twenty-two and turned it over in my hands. I noticed the serial number had been filed off, but that didn't surprise me. It was a common move when you didn't want a traceable gun.

I double-checked the safety then pulled the magazine and cleared the chamber. I held the gun up to the candlelight and looked down the barrel. It was clean and oiled and in excellent condition. I couldn't tell if it'd been fired or not, but with two bullets missing, the answer seemed obvious.

I heard the water turn off in the bathroom, then the shower curtain scrape open. I hurried and put the gun back together then set it on the nightstand just as the bathroom door opened.

Sara came out with her hair wrapped tight in a thin white motel towel. She was carrying the candle in one hand and her clothes in the other. She had another towel wrapped around her chest, and the bottom of it barely reached her legs.

For a moment, watching her cross the room toward me, I forgot all about the storm and all about the money and all about the dead man in my car.

Right then, all I wanted was that towel.

When she got close, I reached for it.

Sara slapped my hand away and said, "Oh my God, no. Are you kidding?"

"What's the problem?"

"Jesus, Nate, a guy died on us tonight and you want to do that?"

"Yeah."

Sara shook her head and dropped her clothes on the bed. She handed me the candle and said, "Not happening."

When I asked her why, she changed the subject.

"What do you think we should do with that money?"

"I've got a few ideas," I said.

"We have a lot to get before the baby comes," Sara said. "I

saw this crib I wanted, but it was almost seven hundred dollars, can you believe it? Who'd pay that kind of money for a crib?"

I set the candle on the nightstand then leaned against the headboard and said, "Lots of people."

"Not me."

"We can afford it."

"No, we can't, Nate." She bent forward and unwrapped the towel around her head and used it to dry her hair as she spoke. "I was thinking that we've got to be careful with what we buy. It'll go quick."

"There's a lot of it. We can get one or two things."

"Like what were you thinking?"

"What about a new car?" I motioned toward the window. "We can get rid of that piece of shit out there."

"We don't need a car," Sara said. "The Dodge runs just fine."

"Don't I get a say in this?"

"Sure you do." Sara sat next to me on the bed then leaned in and kissed me. "But we need to spend it on important things, like a house or a savings account. We can't go out and blow it on a car when we've got a perfectly good one already."

Sara moved and her towel slid farther up her leg, revealing a soft dark patch of hair beneath. I put my hand on her knee then kissed her arm and said, "You're probably right."

I let my hand slide along her leg.

"This money can be a blessing to us, Nate, but we have to be smart about it."

I agreed, kissed her neck.

Sara closed her eyes and leaned back on the bed. When she did, the towel slid away, exposing her breasts, warm and golden in the candlelight.

"Nate, stop."

I didn't, and Sara moved against me.

"You're beautiful," I said.

"I'm fat." She put her hand on her flat stomach. "I can already tell."

I kissed past her neck to her chest. Sara's breath felt warm and strong against my skin, and I slid my hand along the inside of her thigh, moving slow.

Sara moaned then reached down and grabbed my wrist, stopping me. "No, Nate." She moved out from under me then pushed herself up and off the bed, dragging the towel behind her. "Not now, okay?"

"What's wrong?"

"Nothing's wrong," she said. "Just not yet."

I watched her rewrap the towel around her chest, and I didn't say anything.

"I'm sorry," she said. "It just seems weird with everything that happened tonight. Someone died in our car and we're talking about what we're going to do with his money. It doesn't seem right. Can you understand?"

I told her I could, and the part of me that wasn't disappointed actually did.

Sara took her suitcase and opened it on the floor. "Let me get dressed and dry my hair. Maybe I'll feel different in a little while."

I lay back on the bed and stared up at the ceiling and tried to settle my mind. It was a fight I was losing.

A minute passed, then another, then Sara said, "Nate?"

"Yeah?"

"Is that his?"

I lifted my head. Sara was pointing to Syl's black and plaid suitcase.

"Must be," I said. "I grabbed everything I saw."

Sara was quiet.

I let my head drop back to the pillow and tried to think of anything other than how her skin had felt against mine. It wasn't easy to do.

"Did you look inside?"

I didn't say anything right away.

"Maybe we shouldn't," she said. "Right?"

I sat up slow then crossed the room to the suitcase. I picked it up and dropped it on the bed.

There was weight to it.

"Seriously, Nate, maybe we should just leave it be."

The bag was black canvas trimmed with faded red plaid around the edges. A thick metal zipper ran along the top, and when I reached for it, Sara grabbed my hand.

She didn't say anything.

I looked at her then unzipped the bag and pulled the canvas flap back.

Sara was still holding my hand, but neither of us said anything for a long time. At that moment, nothing else existed.

Eventually, Sara turned toward me.

I saw her out of the corner of my eye. She wasn't smiling or crying or anything. There was no emotion at all, and when she spoke, her voice was perfectly calm.

"How much do you think is there?"

11

It took a while to count, and when I finished I put the last few bundles of cash back in the suitcase and said, "Almost two million, plus what we've got in the backpack."

Sara nodded, didn't speak.

She was sitting on the chair by the table. She'd changed into a pair of green sweatpants and an oversized white T-shirt. Her hair was still wet, but she didn't seem to care about that anymore.

I zipped the flap on the suitcase then set it on the floor and slid it under the bed. My hands were shaking, and I reached for my jacket and took the pack of cigarettes out of the pocket. I tapped one out then lit it using one of the candles.

This time, Sara didn't complain.

I sat on the edge of the bed and rested my arms against my knees and tried to think. The idea of two million dollars made it hard to focus, and all I ended up doing was watching a thin ribbon of smoke trail up from my cigarette and unravel into the air around me.

I'd just counted it, I'd held it in my hands, but I still couldn't believe it was real. Even the possibility of that much money was foreign to me.

For years, growing up, Vincent and I would spend nights sleeping in cars or abandoned houses. There was never any money, and sometimes we'd go days without food.

Back then, twenty dollars seemed like a fortune, and I tried to imagine what Vincent would've thought about two million. It was hard to do, but picturing the look on his face made me smile.

"That's all we have to do," Sara said. "It's easy."

"What's all we have to do?"

"Turn it over to the cops." She nodded, her eyes distant. "We won't have anything, so there won't be any reason to come after us. We'll just keep going like we never met him at all."

"What are you talking about?" I asked. "Why would we give it to the cops?"

"We'll be completely out of it. We'll be safe."

"Sara?"

"The police can deal with it."

"We're not giving this money to the cops."

She looked at me. "We have to."

"No, we don't," I said. "We're going to do what we talked about. We'll tell the police what happened, but we're not going to mention the suitcase or any of the money. We'll give them the backpack with his clothes and tell them it was all he had on him when we picked him—"

"No!" Sara stood up fast, her voice loud. "We can't do that. Things are different now."

"Nothing's different."

"Everything is different." Her voice got louder with each word. "Someone shot him because of this money, and now he's dead. If we keep it, they'll come after us, too."

"Who'll come after us?"

"Whoever owns this money. Whoever killed him."

I held up my hands and tried to calm her down, but she stepped away and backed up against the wall.

"No, Nate."

"Sara, come on." I kept my voice soft. "No one knows he had this money."

"Someone does."

"How do you know?"

"Because someone shot him, Nate, and because he had that damn gun. You said it was an assassin's gun."

"I could be wrong about that." I lied. "But even if I'm not, it doesn't mean—"

"Just stop. This kind of thing happens all the time in movies, and it always ends up bad."

"In movies?"

"He was running from someone because of that money and now he's dead. If we take it then they'll come after us."

"This isn't a movie."

Sara looked away. There were tears on her cheek and she wiped them away with the back of her hand. "That money belongs to someone, and they'll come after it until they find it. For all we know they're right behind us."

That reminded me of the diner and Syl asking if anyone had come in while he was in the bathroom. I didn't think anything of it at the time, and I still didn't.

I wouldn't let myself.

"We can't keep it, Nate, we just can't, okay?"

She was crying, and I let her go on until she'd calmed down enough for me to get close, then I took her hands and said, "All we're doing is talking. There's nothing we can do about any of this tonight, so we have some time to think everything through."

"There's nothing to think through," she said. "This isn't worth getting killed over."

I smiled. "Two million dollars?"

Sara pushed past me, but I wrapped my arm around her waist, stopping her.

"Don't joke about this, Nate."

I told her I was sorry, over and over, and when she believed I was telling the truth she leaned into me and put her head against my chest.

We stood like that for a while then I said, "What if there isn't anyone out there?"

"Nate—"

"Just think about it," I said. "What if there's no one coming?"

"There is, I know there is."

"But what if there's not? What if we end up handing all this money over to the cops for no reason?"

She looked at me like she was about to argue. Instead, she said, "There's no way to know for sure. We just have to assume."

"Why?"

"Because if we turn the money in and we're wrong, at least we're still alive."

"And we lose the money."

"It's better than getting killed. If we keep the money we'll always be looking over our shoulders." She paused. "I don't want to live like that."

"Then help me think of a way to keep it that's safe," I said. "There has to be one."

Sara shook her head. "Once we tell the police about Syl, they'll have our names on record. If someone's looking for the money, all they'll have to do is read the report. We were the last ones to see him alive. It won't be hard to figure out what we did."

She was right. Once the police knew, it would be easy to track us down. Still, I wasn't ready to give in.

I went over all the options I could think of, but none of them felt right. After a while, I got up and walked into the bathroom and dropped my cigarette in the toilet. I watched it circle the bowl for a long time.

When I came back, I thought I had the answer.

Sara was standing at the window and staring out into the darkness. I came up behind her and put my hands on her shoulders.

"I think I have an idea," I said.

I felt her shoulders tense. "Nate," she said. "Please, don't—"

"Hear me out."

She let the curtain close then she turned and looked at me. She wasn't smiling. "I know it's a lot of money, but we can't keep it. We need to let it go and move on."

"Will you listen?"

Sara paused. She looked at me for a moment then sat on the edge of the bed and waited.

I moved one of the chairs over, then sat down and said, "Let's go over our options."

"Nate, come on."

I ignored her.

"You think someone is out there looking for this money, and if we keep it we'll be in danger, right?"

"This is pointless."

"Let me finish."

Sara looked away.

"We also can't keep the money because once the police are involved, we'll be listed in their report and easy to track down."

Sara shook her head. "Just tell me your idea."

I hesitated, then said, "What if we don't tell anyone at all?"

12

When I opened the passenger door, a plate of snow slid off the side of the car and crumpled on the ground by my feet. Inside, the overhead light came on, yellow and bright. I reached in and shut it off then stepped back and looked around to see if anyone was watching.

The wind had died and now the snow dropped straight down, thick and unrelenting, like an endless army of white.

I stood there for a while, until I was sure I was alone, then I reached into the car and pulled the blanket away.

Syl's eyes were closed. He'd slipped to the side, and his mouth hung half open. In the shadow, his lips looked purple and I could see his tongue pressing out from behind his teeth like a swollen dark worm.

I reached down and grabbed his legs then swung them around until his feet hung out the door, then I leaned in and took his arm and pulled him up to sitting. He was heavy, so I ducked low and draped his arm over my neck then lifted him across my shoulders and kicked the car door closed.

I'd seen enough war movies to know how to carry a man, but this was the first time I'd ever done it, and it was harder than it'd looked on the screen.

Syl must've outweighed me by fifty pounds, and by the time I'd made it halfway to the playground, my legs were burning under me. All I wanted was to stop and rest, but I knew if I put him down, picking him up again would be even harder.

I kept moving and tried my best to focus on anything other than the weight on my back.

When I got to the edge of the playground, I stopped and looked out at the field in the distance. There was a single cottonwood tree standing alone in the middle of the snow, and from where I stood, it looked miles away.

I considered dropping him closer, finding a hidden spot in the playground and hoping for the best, but that wasn't an option. In order for things to work, Syl needed to stay hidden for as long as possible.

Under the tree, buried in snow.

The longer he was out of sight, the less chance of someone tracing him back to us. If that meant carrying him all the way through the field to the tree, then that's what I was going to do. I didn't think I'd make it without resting along the way, but I was determined to get past the playground first.

I didn't make it.

Halfway through, I stopped walking and eased Syl to the ground. I knelt next to him and waited for the burn in my legs to pass. When it did, I looked around.

I was surrounded on all sides by snow-covered animal rides. Rabbits, chickens, pigs, and horses, all standing silent and still on thick black industrial springs. There were swings on one end of the playground, and a set of monkey bars on the other, and in the middle was a slide shaped like a giant turtle.

I'd been right after all.

The turtle's legs were thick ladders leading to the top of his shell. His tail was the slide, and on the other end, his head stretched out from his body and hung low over the ground. The turtle's face was scarred and dim, and the eyes were the size of Frisbees. I could tell at one time they'd been painted white, but now they were weatherworn and faded to gray, the color of storm clouds.

I stepped closer then reached out to touch the turtle's face. As I did, a white light passed over the playground. I turned fast then dropped to the ground and pushed myself back, under the shell.

I saw a car pull in from the highway and stop next to the office. The headlights were aimed directly at the playground. I didn't move. My heart was slamming against my ribs, and I closed my eyes and focused on my breathing and tried to stay calm.

Syl was where I'd left him, lying on his side in the snow. The light shone directly on him. All it would take was for someone to look our way, and they'd see him.

I eased myself down to my stomach then inched my way out from under the shell. When I got close to Syl, I reached for his leg and tried to pull him out of the light.

He was too heavy, and it didn't work.

Instead, I pushed him onto his back so he wasn't quite as visible, then I crawled back under the shell and waited.

A few minutes passed, then I heard a car door shut followed by the welcome bells above the office door.

There were several small slots cut along the plastic shell, but when I looked through them I couldn't see anything but the glare from the headlights. I wanted to see what was happening, but I didn't want to take the chance of sticking my head out and being seen, so I stayed where I was and listened.

I don't know how long I waited, but after a while my fingers turned numb and started to ache. I squeezed them together and breathed into them. It helped a little, but I was beginning to worry. The dull pain behind my eyes was getting worse, and I still had a long way to go.

A moment later, I heard the bells again. This time I sat up and looked out through the slots at the parking lot. I saw someone cross through the snow then I heard a car door open and close. It wasn't long before the car backed away and the headlights moved, leaving us in the dark.

When I was sure they were gone, I crawled out and watched the car turn the corner and disappear between the buildings. I pushed myself up and out of the snow then walked toward Syl.

Every muscle in my legs felt stiff and frozen, and it took all the strength I had to lift him again.

Once I had him over my shoulder, I kept going along the same path toward the cottonwood tree in the distance. By the time I was clear of the playground, the snow was almost to my knees and the pain behind my eyes had tightened and turned sharp.

I had to force myself to keep moving.

I knew if I hit a rock or stepped in a ditch and lost my footing, there would be no way I could get back up.

All I could do was focus on each step.

I tried to distract myself by thinking of all the things Sara and I could do with the money. The idea I'd never have to see snow again was comforting, and I imagined standing with Sara on a beach somewhere surrounded by palm trees and blue water. I could see us with the baby, but not a baby, a child, a tan and happy child, running along the sand, chasing seagulls through a warm ocean breeze.

I looked up.

The tree was closer.

I told myself that we could buy a boat and sail out onto the ocean where we'd fish and sit in the sun until our skin turned dark. Then, after sunset, we'd lie together and stare up at the stars spinning clean and white through the night sky.

But most of all, we'd never be cold.

There was a sudden flash of pain behind my eyes. It was clean and bright and it tore through my head like a bullet. I felt my knees buckle, and for one sick, detached second, I thought I was going to go down.

Somehow I managed to stay on my feet, and I stood for a moment, trying to ride it out. Eventually, the pain dulled and began to fade. When I thought it was safe, I started moving again.

I don't know how long I walked, but the next time I looked up, the cottonwood tree was right in front of me.

I ducked under the branches and crossed between several small bushes growing around the base. There weren't many, and most were small and thin, but I was glad to see them. They'd give some extra cover, and that was all we needed. Even if they kept him hidden for one extra day, we'd still be one extra day farther down the road.

I walked around the tree, looking for a good spot to put him down, then my foot hit something loose and it slipped under me. I stumbled but managed to catch myself before I fell. Once I was steady, I stepped back and saw the ravine just beyond the bushes.

It was perfect.

I walked to the edge then turned and let Syl drop off my shoulder to the ground. He hit hard, then rolled into the ravine and sunk facedown into the snow at the bottom.

A second later, I heard him moan.

I stood on the edge, unable to move.

I told myself that I'd imagined the sound, that it was only the wind, but I knew it wasn't true. There was no wind, just slow falling snow.

I stayed there for a long time, under the tree, staring at him at the bottom of the ravine, and listening.

Then he coughed.

Now I was far away, watching from a distance.

I saw Syl try to turn himself over, but he couldn't do it, and he moaned again.

The sound was sad, panicked.

I saw myself step forward and slide down into the ravine. The snow at the bottom went up to my knees, and I struggled through it. Once I got close, I reached out to him then stopped.

I didn't know what I was going to do.

The ravine was deep and I didn't have the strength left to pull him out. Even if I could've, I knew there was no way I'd be able to carry him all the way back to the motel.

It was too late.

There was nothing I could do.

Syl was breathing hard, moaning, trying to turn over. I told myself I had to go, that I had to climb out and walk away, but I couldn't move.

I couldn't leave him, not like that.

I stepped closer and pulled him over onto his back.

When I did, he looked right at me, his eyes distant and unfocused. He turned his head from one side to the other before coming back to me. This time I saw a flash of clarity on his face, then understanding, then fear.

"I know you," he said.

His voice was dry and thin.

I backed away.

The pain in my head was blinding.

Syl lifted one hand and tried to say something else, but all that came out was a long rush of air.

I started climbing out of the ravine.

Syl cried out, his hand shook.

I kept climbing.

When I got to the top, I could hear him shuffling around, trying to speak, trying to sit up. Once again, I told myself there was nothing I could do, that he was too far gone to help. I told myself I had to keep going, that he wasn't going to make it no matter what I did.

I wasn't sure if that was true or not, but it was enough to get me moving again.

As I walked away, I could hear him coughing but I didn't look back. Sometimes I'd hear him crying out to me in that weak, dry voice, and every time he did, I felt something shrink inside me.

I tried to focus on Sara and the baby. I told myself I had to do what was right for them, that they were counting on me, and that I had to be strong.

No matter what, I had to be strong.

When I got far enough away I stopped and looked back at the tree and watched it lean and sway under the weight of the snow.

It was my last chance.

I knew if I didn't do something, Syl was going to freeze out there. If I didn't help, it would be the same as if I'd held a gun to his head and pulled the trigger.

In my heart I knew that I couldn't leave him out there to die, that it wasn't inside me, it wasn't who I was.

But in the end, that's exactly what I did.

13

I followed my footprints out of the field, and by the time I reached the edge of the playground I could barely stand up. The pain behind my eyes screamed through me, making it almost impossible to stay on my feet.

I could see the turtle up ahead, and I locked on to it and forced myself to move forward. When I got to it, I stopped and leaned against its shell. I felt my legs wobble under me and then a forest of black flowers bloomed behind my eyes. The world spun and I turned to the side and vomited into the snow.

It scared me enough to keep moving.

When I walked out of the playground, my foot hit something buried in the snow and I fell forward. I tried to push myself up, but there was no strength in my arms.

I stayed there, facedown, listening to my breathing, and feeling the snow burn numb against my skin.

I closed my eyes, and all I could think about was Vincent, and that it should've been me.

I don't know how much time passed, but when I looked up I could see the corner of our building through the snow.

It was so close.

I pushed myself up enough to get my legs under me, then I stood and staggered the rest of the way through the parking lot. When I reached our building, I stopped and leaned against the side.

Dark shadows crept in from the corners of my vision, and I leaned forward and waited for them to pass. When they did, I inched along the wall to our room.

Once I got to the door, I saw a tiny red light floating in the air across the parking lot. At first, I thought it was my vision playing tricks on me, then the light got brighter, and I saw a man's face in the glow.

I didn't understand what I was seeing, then the red light flew into the air and landed soft in the snow.

A cigarette.

A second later, the door across the parking lot opened and someone went inside. I stood for a moment, hoping that what I saw wasn't real, but I knew it was.

Someone had been watching.

———

Sara opened the door and stepped back.

"Oh, God!"

I went inside, then straight to my bag by the side of the bed. I grabbed my pills and tried to open them but my fingers were frozen and I couldn't work the lid.

Sara took the bottle and tapped two pills into her palm then handed them to me.

I swallowed them dry then said, "More."

She tapped out two more.

I took them, then sat on the edge of the bed.

"Are you okay?"

She kept her voice soft. She knew.

I told her I was, then leaned forward and tried to untie the laces on my boots. They were caked with snow and ice, and my fingers wouldn't bend.

"Get my boots."

Sara bent down and knocked the snow away then untied the laces. She pulled off my boots then my socks. They were soaked through, and my feet were numb.

I tried to stand.

"What are you doing?"

"Bath," I said.

She helped me up then grabbed one of the candles from the nightstand.

"No light."

"It's just a candle."

"No light."

Right then, any light was too much.

Sara put the candle down then helped me to the bathroom. Once I was inside, she asked if I needed help.

I told her I could do it.

She stood in the doorway for a moment longer, then she stepped out and shut the door.

With the door closed, the bathroom was black except for

a small frosted window, high up next to the ceiling. The light leaking through the glass was cold and gray, like a dying moon.

I leaned down and turned the water to hot then started taking off the rest of my clothes. When I was naked, I crawled over the side and sat in the tub and let the water cover me.

I kept my eyes closed until the stabbing pain in my head started to fade, then I looked up and focused on the window, hanging in the steam.

The water burned my skin, but I still couldn't stop shivering. I could feel the familiar haze that came along with my pills. It pulled at me, removing me from the world one step at a time.

I welcomed it.

Once my headache was gone, I closed my eyes and slid under the water. The silence was glorious, and I felt like I could hold my breath forever.

———

When I opened my eyes again, the water had turned cold. I reached over and pulled the plug on the drain then got up and grabbed one of the towels off the rack and wrapped it around my waist.

I stepped out, bracing myself against the sink.

The room was dark and the tile floor felt cold and slick under my feet. I stood for a while, staring at my reflection in the mirror, but all I could see was a shadow, hunched forward, breathing.

Every time I closed my eyes I saw Syl's face staring up at me from the bottom of the ravine. Someone told me once that freezing wasn't a bad way to die, that eventually your brain just shut down and you fell asleep.

Nice and peaceful.

I wanted to believe it was true.

I grabbed the sides of the sink and squeezed. I could feel my pulse in my jaw, and I knew the pain in my head was still there, hidden under my medication, waiting.

The image of Syl wouldn't go away.

I could still hear his voice, calling for me to help.

I wondered if he was already dead.

His voice got louder. I couldn't escape it.

I bit the insides of my cheeks, hard, then stepped back and slammed my fist against the mirror. The glass shattered and dug into my knuckles, but there was no pain.

Syl's voice was gone.

I stood for a moment, breathing hard, my heart beating strong in my chest. I could feel blood running over my hand and dripping onto the tile floor.

Somewhere far away, Sara was calling me.

I reached down and opened the door.

She was sitting up in bed, naked, and when she saw me she said, "What happened? Are you okay?"

I didn't answer. Instead, I crossed the room and climbed on top of her, pushing her back on the bed.

"Nate?"

I kissed her.

She fought me at first, then she kissed me back.

I reached down and moved her legs apart.

"Wait, your hand. You're bleeding."

I held her down and pressed into her.

Sara inhaled, sharp, and dug her nails into the back of my neck. I drove into her, hard, over and over.

I felt her breath against my skin, hot and sweet.

"It's ours, isn't it?" she said. "It's all ours."

There were tears on my face, running down, mixing with my blood, covering us both.

I closed my eyes.

"Yes," I said. "It's all ours."

She moaned, and her legs squeezed tight around me.

I thought about the ocean.

I thought about blue skies and lazy palm trees leaning softly into a smooth yellow sun. I thought about warm nights on an empty beach, Sara next to me, staring up at a shatter of stars.

We had more money than I'd ever imagined.

We could do anything we wanted.

We were free.

Yet I couldn't stop crying.

Part II

14

I woke up sweating.

Someone was knocking on the door.

I sat up and tried to clear my head. My heart was beating hard, and I could taste something sour at the back of my throat.

The knocking came again, louder this time.

Sara rolled over and said, "Who is that?"

I started to tell her I didn't know, then she pushed the covers away and ran toward the bathroom with her hand over her mouth. I didn't think she was going to make it in time, but she did.

Whoever was outside knocked again.

I looked at the gun on the nightstand then got up and reached for my pants on the floor. I took the gun and slid it into the back of my belt then opened the door.

Butch was standing outside, smiling.

"Good morning, Minnesota," he said.

He had on a ripped red flannel jacket and a red hunter's cap with earflaps. There was a wrinkled cigarette in his mouth and he smiled around it.

"How'd you sleep?"

"No complaints," I said.

"Good to hear."

I looked past him and saw the snow had been cleared off the parking lot. I asked him about it.

"Half of it, anyway." Butch pointed to the building across from us and said, "My nephew has one of those snowplow attachments for his pickup. The idiot ran it into one of the concrete parking barriers and snapped the damn mounting." He shook his head. "Surprised you didn't hear it. I thought he was gonna wake the dead."

"Your nephew is staying over there?"

"Lives there," Butch said. "He's lived here, on and off, since he was a kid. Helps me out around the place, day-to-day maintenance, that kind of thing."

I thought about the man I saw standing out there the night before, smoking his cigarette, watching me. I still wanted to believe I'd imagined it all, but I couldn't.

"Anywhoo." Butch took another drag off the cigarette then flicked it into the snow. "I stopped by to let you folks know the road is still closed. That's the bad news. The good news is that I put together a breakfast over in the office. Everyone's invited. We've got a small kitchen with a few tables and chairs set up. The food ain't much, but we got enough to get us by."

Behind me, the sound of Sara throwing up carried through the thin bathroom door.

Butch frowned.

"How's your friend holding up?"

It took me a moment, then it came to me.

I smiled.

"She's better than she was last night," I said. "Didn't need a hospital after all."

"Well, that's good."

"You must've been right," I said. "A good night's sleep seemed to help."

"It's amazing how often it does."

He stood at the door for another minute, neither of us speaking, then he thumbed back over his shoulder and said, "Well, I need to keep spreading the word."

"You get a lot of people in last night?"

He shook his head. "Four or five, including you two."

"Is that a lot?"

"These days it is," he said. "We used to do our share during hunting season, but not so much anymore. Now, most folks stay at one of the big chains over in Harlan or back in Red Oak."

"Sorry to hear it."

"It is what it is," he said. "You know what they say, time and tide."

I didn't know, but I kept that to myself.

I watched Butch fish another wrinkled cigarette out of his pocket and light it with a kitchen match, then he waved it out and said, "Hope to see you two at breakfast, if she's feeling up to it, of course."

I told him he would, then he turned and walked away.

I closed the door.

Sara was still in the bathroom, so I sat on the bed and waited. I noticed the green backpack lying on the floor by the bed. Seeing it made me think of Syl, which made me wonder. Soon my hands were shaking, and I squeezed them together as tight as I could.

They wouldn't stop.

A few minutes later I heard the toilet flush and the water run in the sink, then Sara came out holding one hand over her stomach.

"I hope this doesn't last the entire time," she said.

"Is it supposed to get better?"

"I think so."

She climbed back into bed and pulled the covers up to her chin. "Who was at the door?"

I told her about the food.

"Ugh, stop."

"Not hungry?"

"God, no."

"Probably just bananas and wet vending machine muffins," I said. "I'm hoping for coffee."

"Jesus, Nate, knock it off, will you?"

I kept talking, but I had no idea why.

The words just seemed to roll out of my mouth. I ran through all the breakfast foods I could think of, eggs and bacon, omelets, waffles, pancakes and maple syrup.

The list went on and on.

I didn't stop until I felt Sara's hands on my face. When I looked up, she was sitting on her knees, holding my head between her hands. Her eyes were soft, worried.

"I'm sorry," I said. "I don't know what's wro—"

She shushed me then leaned in and kissed me, soft. I didn't want her to stop, but eventually she did.

"Are you okay?"

I nodded, but this time there were no words.

"Are you sure?"

I told her I was.

"The worst part is over," she said. "It's done."

I watched her, and for a second the desire to tell her what'd happened the night before was overwhelming. I even opened my mouth and started to confess, but I stopped myself and looked away. I knew I'd tell her someday, but not yet. She'd had a hard enough time when she thought Syl had died in the car. She wasn't ready to know the truth.

Sara kissed me again and I turned away.

I reached for my shoes on the floor and slid them on, then grabbed my jacket off the back of the chair.

"Nate?"

"Yeah?"

"Are you sure you're okay?"

"I'm fine."

She paused. "Was it really awful?"

I told her it was, then motioned to the door. "Are you sure you don't want me to bring you some food?"

She didn't say anything right away, then she leaned back and pulled the sheet up around her neck and said, "Something light, a banana or an apple, maybe? In case I'm hungry later."

I told her I'd see what I could find, then I opened the door and stepped out into the cold.

I pulled my jacket tight and started down the walkway toward the office. When I got to the end of the building, I looked out at the empty field. I could see the cottonwood tree in the distance. It stood black and skeletal, a thin crack against a white sky.

I stared at it for a while, thinking about the night before and trying to ignore the cold feeling spreading through my chest. When I finally turned away, I told myself that what was done was done, and it couldn't be taken back. I had to let it go.

Syl was dead, and the snow was deep.

It would be a long time before anyone found him, and with any luck, the plows were already on their way. We'd be back on the road this afternoon.

All we had to do was wait.

By the time I got to the office, my hands had stopped shaking. I'd managed to convince myself that everything was okay, that I'd done what was right for Sara and the baby, and that things were going to work out. I even stood outside the office and listened for the low scraping groan of the plows that I was sure were on the way.

Instead, all I heard was the thin, cold hiss of the wind passing over snow.

15

Once inside the office, I could smell fresh coffee and fried bacon. There was a piece of paper taped to the front desk with the words "Dining Room" written in thick black letters and an arrow pointing toward an open door at the far end of the room.

I walked through.

There were several folding tables set up around a large brick fireplace. The fire burning inside was warm and smelled like autumn. The only people I saw were an older couple playing cards at one table, and a girl in a black hooded sweatshirt at another. She was holding an empty coffee cup with both hands and staring out the window at the snow.

They all looked up when I walked in.

There was a lime green refrigerator along the far wall and a gas stove with a blue metal coffeepot bubbling on one of the burners. Next to it, on the counter, was a large plate stacked with scrambled eggs and bacon.

No fruit.

I took a step toward the food, then hesitated.

The older woman looked at me over the thickest glasses I'd ever seen and said, "Help yourself, honey. Butch stepped out for a minute, but he'll be right back. You met Butch, right?"

I told her I had.

The man across from her made a dismissive sound then said, "We think he runs the place." He didn't look up from his cards. "He might even own it, but who the hell knows."

The old woman frowned and shook her head. The gesture was both disapproving and apologetic. It made me smile and imagine how Sara and I would be in forty years.

"I think he owns it," I said. "That's the impression he gave me."

The old man didn't say anything else, so I walked past him and went straight for the coffee. There were mugs on the counter. I picked one up then reached for the pot.

"Watch yourself," the woman said. "You'll lose your fingerprints." She pointed to a hot pad on the counter. "Use that. You'll thank me."

I picked up the hot pad and used it to grab the handle. Even with it, I could feel the heat.

I took one of the paper plates off the counter and spooned out some eggs and a few pieces of bacon then sat at one of the empty tables.

The eggs were good. The coffee was brilliant.

"You've never used one before, have you?"

I looked up at the woman. "Never used what?"

"A percolator," she said. "The coffee."

I shook my head.

"Neither of you." She motioned to the girl by the window. "I suppose you're both too young. Marcus and I keep one around for camping, in case we want to make coffee over a fire, but you don't see them too often anymore."

"Except here," Marcus said. "Probably never heard of Mr. Coffee."

"And Mr. Coffee works great with no electricity, doesn't it?" the woman said. "There's something to be said about the old way of doing things, and you should count your blessings." She looked back at me. "Can you believe how fast that storm hit? What time did you get in?"

I told her I didn't know, then added, "Late."

"Us, too," she said. "He's not happy about being here, but I don't mind. This place reminds me of being a kid. It's like a snapshot of the past."

I looked around the room. All four walls were rimmed with wainscoting and several dusty paintings of farms and Midwestern sunsets. The ceiling was spotted with water stains, and the carpet was faded and thin.

"You by yourself?"

"My fiancée is in our room," I said. "She's not feeling too good."

"Sorry to hear it," the woman said. "My name is Caroline, by the way. This is my husband, Marcus."

Marcus tapped the side of his head with one crooked finger then took several blue and white poker chips from a stack in front of him and pushed them into the middle of the table and said, "Raise."

Caroline ignored him. "That's Megan over there. She came in late, after they closed the road." Caroline leaned close and whispered, "She's over here from Russia, studying to be a doctor."

I nodded, then turned toward her and smiled. Megan smiled

back, but didn't seem to care if we met or not. I didn't either, but I figured it was good to be polite.

"I'm Nate," I said. "Sara is back in the room."

"Nothing serious, I hope."

"No, she's okay."

"That's good." She motioned to my hand and frowned. "That looks like it hurt."

"Not too bad."

I'd used the gauze in Syl's bag to wrap my hand the night before, but now several dark stains were blossoming on the surface. I made a mental note to change it when I got back to the room.

"Are you going to take her some food when you go?" Caroline asked. "Food sometimes helps."

"Carol," Marcus said. "Why don't you just play your damn hand and stop talking the man's ear off while he's trying to eat?"

"Why don't you butt out?" Caroline looked at me, her eyes swollen behind her lenses. "Am I bugging you, Nate? If I am, I'm sorry."

"I don't mind."

She turned back to Marcus. "You know I'm going to beat you anyway, so why do you care?" She dropped a stack of chips into the middle of the table then turned her cards faceup in front of her. "Now, why don't you grab me some more coffee, can you do that?"

Marcus looked from his cards to hers then grunted and pushed himself away from the table. He took her cup and crossed the room toward the stove, mumbling to himself.

"Marcus retired this year," she said. "He's not taking it very well, especially now, with the markets the way they are."

I nodded like I understood. I couldn't think of anything better than not having to work.

Maybe that was just me.

Marcus yelled, then I heard the coffeepot hit the burner. "Mother, fu—, goddamn it."

Caroline shook her head. She was smiling. "Use the hot pad, sweetheart."

"Thank you, dear," he said.

She reached out and touched my arm. Her hand was soft, and I couldn't help but like her. "Marcus is a poet," she said. "A good one, too."

"Is that right?"

"Marcus, read him one of your poems."

"He doesn't want to hear one of my poems."

"And how do you know that? He might love poetry."

Marcus came back to the table with Caroline's coffee cup. He set it in front of her then looked at me.

"Do you love poetry, Nate?"

I told him I didn't know much about poetry.

He looked at Caroline. "See? What did I tell you?"

Caroline frowned. "Well, if you're too embarrassed."

Marcus muttered something under his breath, then sat down and took a silver flask from his jacket pocket and opened the top. "I can't win."

He held the flask over his cup and poured a shot into his coffee, then reached across the table and poured another into Caroline's.

"I'll keep working on him," Caroline said. "He'll read one before the highway reopens, you'll see."

Marcus sat back and Caroline tapped the rim of her coffee cup. "Don't be stingy now."

Marcus handed her the flask and she held it out to me.

"Would you like a drink, Nate?"

I shook my head then watched her pour another shot into her coffee before setting the flask on the table.

"If you change your mind, just say the word."

I told her I would then went back to my eggs.

I'd finished them all by the time Butch came into the room. He had a plastic cooler with two loaves of bread sitting on top.

"This is all of it," he said. "I'll leave what we don't eat in this cooler then set it out back in the snow so it doesn't spoil. Never know when the refrigerator will work again."

"Hear anything about the roads?" Marcus asked.

"Afraid not," Butch said. "Radio says we've got more snow coming tonight."

"Are you sure?"

Butch nodded. "It's not looking good out there."

I didn't want to believe it, so I chose not to. Instead, I finished my coffee then got up to get more.

Butch was pulling food out of the refrigerator and stacking it in the cooler. When he saw me, he said, "Good to see you, Minnesota. How's your friend feeling?"

"Sick," I said. "I was going to take her a plate, if you don't mind."

"Don't mind a bit. Help yourself." He looked around the counter. "I should have some foil someplace. We can wrap it up so it doesn't freeze before you get it to her."

I reached for one of the paper plates but Butch stopped me and took a real plate from the counter.

"Easier to carry," he said. "That one will fall apart halfway back to your room."

I took it then started spooning out eggs and bacon. She'd go for the bacon, but I didn't think she'd want to look at the eggs, much less eat them. Still, I wanted to give her the option. If she didn't want them, I'd eat 'em.

Butch found the foil and handed it to me.

I wrapped the plate then thanked him.

"Don't mention it," he said. "Just make sure to bring it back when you're finished, if you don't mind."

I told him I would, then I slid my coat on and said good-bye to Caroline and Marcus.

On my way out, I passed Megan at the table.

She didn't look at me, and as I walked by, I noticed several jagged scars running along her wrists.

I kept walking, pretending I never saw them.

16

Someone had shoveled the walkways around the buildings, so the trek back to the room was easier. I tried to hurry, but I knew it wouldn't matter. The eggs were going to be cold.

I crossed through the parking lot toward our room. When I got close, I heard a man's voice, then the sound of Sara laughing.

No, not laughing, giggling.

"Believe it or not," the man said. "It's the truth."

More giggling.

I turned the corner and stopped.

Sara was standing in the doorway to our room. She had her robe on and was holding it closed with both hands.

The man had his back to me, but I knew who he was even without seeing his face.

Sara saw me and tried to smile.

I could see the worry in her eyes.

"Hey, Nate," she said. "This is our neighbor, Zack. He works here."

Zack turned and looked at me. He held out his hand. "There's the man, right there."

I hesitated, then shook his hand.

His skin felt rough and damp.

"Good to meet you," he said.

I looked past him to Sara.

She shrugged.

"I was out clearing the snow and decided to introduce myself," he said. "Got to talking with your girlfriend and lost the time."

"Fiancée."

"What?"

"Fiancée," I said. "Not girlfriend."

Zack stared at me for a moment then his lips slid sideways into a smile, showing a scatter of tobacco yellow teeth. "My mistake."

"It's no big deal," Sara said. "Is it, Nate."

"Nope," I said. "No big deal."

Zack didn't look away from me, and the smile never broke. "That's a hell of a scrape you got," he said. "How'd you get it?"

I touched the scar on my forehead. "Long story."

Zack's eyes narrowed. "I'm sure it is."

For a moment, no one spoke, then Sara said, "Zack's uncle owns the place."

"Butch?"

"All it means is I get stuck doing the work he doesn't want to do. The list gets longer every year, too."

"He seems active enough."

"When he wants to be," Zack said. "He pretends he's old

and frail, but he's not. Believe me, that son of a bitch is going to hang around forever."

"Do you live here full-time?" Sara asked.

"I do," he said. "You can't beat free rent, at least not in this life."

Sara looked at me. "Zack was telling me about some of the crazy things he's seen around here."

"That so?"

"Tell him about that couple with the baby dolls."

Zack dragged the shovel along the sidewalk and the sound echoed under the walkway. "I don't want to keep you two out in the cold. Maybe we'll have time to talk later on. It looks like you'll be stuck here for a while."

"Why would we be stuck here?" Sara looked at me. "What's going on?"

I told her about the radio and the storm coming.

"What about the plows—"

"We'll see what happens."

Zack watched us. "You two in a hurry?"

"Just want to keep moving." I handed the plate to Sara. "Eggs and bacon, probably cold by now. Think you can keep them down?"

She took them, didn't speak.

"Are you sick?" Zack asked.

Sara looked at him then shrugged. "Just pregnant."

Zack's eyes went wide. "Is that right? Well, God bless you, that's wonderful."

Sara smiled, and for the first time in days I saw color in her cheeks.

"It's not so wonderful right now," she said. "He's doing a number on my stomach."

"No, it's a blessing," Zack said. "Any time God brings a child into the world it's a blessing."

"If you say so."

"Oh, I do. And what's more, so does He."

Sara looked up at me. I could tell she'd had enough.

I stepped forward and said, "Listen, we're going to—"

"Right," Zack said. "I should get back to work and let you two get on with your day." He held out his hand and I shook it again. "You and I need to get together and have a drink, celebrate the child." He motioned toward his room. "I got a bottle of Johnny Walker up there. We can go to work on it later."

"Thanks, but we're hoping to—"

"I'll tell you some of the crazy things I've seen around here lately, and you can tell me about that scar."

He looked at me and something passed between us.

I paused. "Sure, why not."

Zack turned to Sara. "You're welcome to join us, without the drink, of course."

"Not this time," she said. "Thanks."

"Suit yourself." Zack picked up the snow shovel and started down the walkway. When he got to the bottom, he stopped and took in a deep breath then said, "I have a feeling it's gonna be a glorious day."

———

Once we were both inside with the door closed, Sara started asking me about the plows and the coming storm. I barely heard her. We had bigger problems.

"How bad is it supposed to be?"

"What?"

"The storm," Sara said. "Did they say—"

"I don't know. It doesn't matter."

"Doesn't matter? Nate, we can't be stuck here."

"We might not have a choice," I said. "And another day or two isn't going to make a difference. The more snow we get, the longer it'll take to find him. By the time they do, we'll be long gone."

Sara sat on the edge of the bed. "I'll feel better when we're on the road."

"Yeah," I said. "Me, too."

We didn't talk for a while, then Sara looked at me and said, "You look worried."

"I am." I motioned toward the window. "He knows."

"No, he doesn't."

"He saw me last night."

Sara was quiet. "Are you sure?"

I went over everything, leaving out the part about Syl in the ravine. When I finished, I said, "This is bad."

Sara folded her hands in front of her mouth and closed her eyes. When she opened them again she said, "Did you see him on your way out?"

I told her I didn't.

"So, he only saw you when you were coming back."

"Maybe, I can't be sure."

"Be sure, Nate."

Her voice was harsh.

I thought about it for a moment.

I'd taken my time getting Syl out of the car. If anyone had been outside, I would've seen them.

"Okay," I said. "I'm sure."

"So all he saw was you walking outside."

"In a blizzard."

"That's not against the law."

"It's strange."

"You should've heard some of the stories he was telling me." She smiled. "Walking around in a blizzard is nothing compared to what he's seen."

I wanted to feel better, but I didn't. Zack knew something was going on. He might not have seen everything that happened last night, but he'd seen enough to come over and try to make me nervous. And he did a good job.

"I'll find out for sure when I talk to him."

"You're going over there?"

"I have to. I have to know."

"I wish you wouldn't," she said. "That guy makes me nervous. You should've seen how he was looking at me."

"I need to find out what he saw last night. Maybe it's nothing."

Sara thought about it for a moment, then nodded. "I guess you're right."

Neither of us spoke for a while, then I said, "You know he has a meth lab set up out back?"

"Seriously?"

"In a pig shed behind the building."

"How do you know it's a meth lab?"

I told her about the open door slamming in the wind and about seeing him come out of the shed. Then I told her how I'd walked over to close the door and what I'd found inside.

"Fireworks?"

"Bags of them," I said. "They use the red phosphorus inside of 'em."

"That's disgusting."

"That's nothing. You wouldn't believe what goes into that shit."

"Do you think we should tell somebody?"

I laughed.

"What's so funny?"

"We're not getting involved. Whatever's going on around here is none of our business."

Sara didn't say anything.

"We have to lay low until that road opens," I said. "No one knows us, and we need to keep it that way. I don't even think the owner remembers my name. He keeps calling—"

I stopped, my throat felt tight.

"What's wrong?"

"The notebook," I said. "When we checked in last night the computer was down. Butch wrote my name and address in a notebook."

Sara stared at me.

"I didn't know."

"Did you see where he kept it?"

"On a shelf under the front desk."

"Can you get it back?"

There was no other option.

Butch had written down everything, my address, my driver's license number, all of it. If the cops wanted to find us, that notebook would point the way.

I had to get it back.

Sara asked if I was sure I could do it.

I told her I was.

"I don't have a choice."

17

Sara didn't bother trying to eat.

I took the plate and scraped the eggs and bacon into the ice bucket then reached for my coat.

"What are you going to do?"

"Don't know yet."

"Don't get caught."

I told her I'd do my best, then I picked up the empty plate and walked out toward the office. On the way, I heard the rough scrape of Zack's snow shovel on concrete.

It sounded far away, and I was glad.

When I got to the office, Butch was standing behind the desk, spinning the dial on the radio. He looked up as I walked in then said, "Back for more?"

"Hope it's not too much trouble."

"It's no trouble at all," he said. "I don't believe we're to the point of rationing just yet."

I glanced toward the dining room.

"Go on, help yourself."

Sara wasn't going to eat anything I brought back, but I needed a reason. I had to stick around long enough to grab the notebook, and I figured this was as good an excuse as any.

I thanked him and went in.

The room was exactly how I'd left it. Megan was still at the table with her coffee, and Caroline and Marcus were still playing their game, silent, staring at their cards.

The silver flask was sitting open in front of Marcus.

I walked past them to the counter and set the plate next to the eggs.

"She feeling better?"

I looked up at Caroline. "Excuse me?"

"Your girl," she said. "How's she feeling?"

"Better, I think."

"That's good." She motioned toward the plate. "Is that for her?"

I nodded. "She's getting her appetite back at least."

"That's a good sign." Caroline patted the table next to her, and when she spoke I could hear the slow slur deep in her voice. "Why don't you sit and play a hand. I could use some real competition for once."

Marcus didn't look up, just shook his head, kept quiet.

"Then you don't want me," I said. "I'm not a good gambler. I always lose."

"So says the shark."

"This time it's the truth."

"Lucky for you, it's not real money," Caroline said. "We're just playing for fun. Do you like poker?"

"Sure, I guess."

"Then have a seat and I'll deal you in."

"Thanks," I said. "But I can't. I need to get back."

"Well, maybe later," Caroline said. "We're all going to be here for a while. The game will continue."

"I hope you're wrong about that," I said. "I'd like to get back on the road."

"Amen." Marcus looked up from his cards and shouted toward the office, "What's the word on the weather, Butch?"

I heard Butch shuffle around in the other room, then a minute later he came in carrying the radio.

"Signal's no good in there. I'll try it in here."

He set it on the counter and adjusted the antenna. There was a buzz of static. Butch turned the dial and a flat voice began talking about the sin of Cain.

"They do news and weather on this station about every hour or so. We'll keep it here, as long as no one minds listening to the reverend in between."

No one said anything.

While Butch was at the counter, I asked him if I could use the aluminum foil again.

"Take what you need."

I tore off a sheet then said, "I met your nephew this morning."

Butch stopped adjusting the antenna and looked at me. "Zack? Where?"

"Shoveling the walks," I said. "He was talking to my fiancée when I got back."

"He was in your room?"

"Outside, in the doorway."

Butch frowned. "I'll have a talk with him."

"It's not a big deal," I said. "I wasn't trying to get him in trouble."

"He knows he's not supposed to talk to the guests," Butch said. "If he comes by again, you tell me."

There was something in his voice I didn't like, and it made me think of the shed and the meth lab inside.

"Is there a problem?"

"What do you mean?"

"The way you're talking about him. You make it sound like he's dangerous."

"Zack?" Butch smiled, but it wasn't convincing. "No, of course not. He just has an interesting way of looking at the world, and sometimes it makes people uncomfortable."

"What do you mean?"

Butch waved me off. "It's not important. Just let me know if he bothers you again and I'll take care of it." He put his hand on my shoulder and tapped it twice. "Nothing to worry about."

I started to say something else, but Butch turned toward Caroline and Marcus and said, "You two got room for one more?"

"Have a seat," Caroline said. "New blood is always welcome."

Butch walked around the table and sat down.

On the radio, the reverend went on, each word louder than the last: "'And the Lord set a mark upon Cain, lest any finding him should kill him. And Cain went out from the presence of the lord, and dwelt in the land of Nod, on the east of Eden.'"

Megan got up and grabbed her coat off her chair and started for the door.

It seemed like a good idea.

I finished wrapping the plate of food and followed her out. On the way, I told Caroline I'd be back for that game in a while.

"We'll be here," she said. "Bring your girl along next time, if she's feeling up to it."

I told her I would, then I walked out of the dining room and into the office. I stopped at the front desk and set the plate on the counter then zipped my coat. I could hear the voices in the other room, and when I felt like it was safe, I slid in behind the desk.

The first thing I saw was a twin-barrel shotgun leaning against the wall.

I hesitated.

Seeing the gun stopped me for a minute, but I wasn't sure why. It was logical to have a gun, especially out here in the middle of nowhere. You never knew what kind of people were out on the road.

I started searching.

There were two shelves behind the desk. The top one was stacked with paper towels and a spray bottle filled with a light green liquid. The next shelf had a series of receipt books, magazines, and newspaper crosswords.

I picked up the magazines and shuffled through the titles. Most were familiar, *Guns & Ammo, Soldier of Fortune.*

Some weren't.

I stopped at one with a picture of three young men on the cover. They were standing together in their underwear with their arms around each other, smiling into the camera.

Above them, in bold letters, was the word TWINKS.

At first I thought it was a catalog.

I opened it and flipped through the pages.

I was wrong.

Behind me, I heard Caroline laugh and Butch say, "Well, I'll be damned." Then the thin rattle of chips sliding across the table.

I looked up to see if anyone was coming, then I put the magazines back on the shelf. When I did, I saw the notebook sitting next to a stack of paper towels.

I heard a chair slide across the dining room floor.

I grabbed the notebook and flipped through it until I found my name, then I tore the page out and stuffed it in my pocket.

I put the notebook back and stood up.

Butch was standing in the doorway.

For a moment, neither of us said anything.

"Help you with something, Minnesota?"

My throat felt tight, but I managed to find my voice.

"Matches," I said. "We ran out."

Butch stared at me then pointed to a box of kitchen matches on the shelf next to the wooden pegboard. "Take what you need."

I took a few, thanked him, then came around to the front of the desk.

"Anything else you're after?"

I told him there wasn't.

Butch walked behind the desk and looked around, then stared up at me. He didn't speak.

I grabbed the plate off the desk and thanked him again for the matches then turned toward the door.

Butch stopped me.

"Do me a favor, Minnesota."

"What's that?"

"Next time you want something, just ask."

I told him I would.

When I opened the door and walked out, my head was throbbing. I told myself I'd make it up to Butch and leave some money in the room to cover the cost of our stay.

I'd even leave a couple hundred extra for the mirror and the inconvenience.

I didn't mind.

Butch seemed like a decent guy.

———

The sky outside was a cold white haze. I could see the sun working behind the clouds, but it wasn't cutting through. There was no sign of the plows, but no sign of another storm, either, and that was a good thing.

With luck, the plows were on their way.

Things were looking up.

I'd managed to get the page from the notebook, and for the first time that day, I allowed myself to relax. We'd covered ourselves the best we could, and now it was out of our hands. All we could do was wait.

I started across the parking lot toward our building. The plate of food was hot and I switched it from one hand to the other as I walked. Then, when I turned the corner, I noticed something dark lying at the edge of the playground.

At first I thought it was a blanket or maybe a trash bag blown in with the storm, but something about it didn't look right.

I started across the parking lot toward the playground. When I got closer I saw what it was and felt something cold spread through my chest.

It wasn't a blanket or a trash bag, it was a man.

It was Syl.

I stood where I was, unable to move.

I didn't believe what I was seeing, and that gave me the strength to start walking again.

I had to be sure.

When I got close, I looked at him lying facedown in the snow. His coat was ripped and his pants were caked with mud. One shoe was missing, and the sock was pushed down past his ankle, showing a band of blue skin.

I couldn't tell if he was alive or not, and I couldn't bring myself to check. The last thing I wanted to do was touch him.

I stood over him, unable to accept it.

The plate I was carrying burned my hand, and I dropped it in the snow.

The pain brought me back.

I knelt down then reached out to turn him over. When I did, I noticed the tracks behind him. Not footprints, but two deep grooves leading back into the field, as if he'd dragged himself through the snow.

That wasn't possible.

I couldn't imagine him pulling himself out of the ravine, much less dragging himself all the way back to the motel in the middle of a blizzard.

It didn't make sense.

I got up and walked past him so I could take a closer look at the grooves in the snow. When I did, I saw the footprints staggered along the side.

He hadn't dragged himself back.

Someone else had.

I went back to Syl and stared at him for a moment longer, then I looked down at the overturned plate and the bright yellow eggs, scattered and steaming in the snow.

I thought about Sara and wondered what I was going to tell her.

She didn't deserve what was coming.

18

I heard someone behind me, and when I looked back I saw Megan running across the parking lot. She approached slowly, and when she got close, I stepped away from Syl.

"Did you see where he came from?"

I didn't answer at first, and she asked me again.

This time I shook my head.

My thoughts split and trailed away in several directions. If someone had dragged him back, then someone had seen me carry him out.

It didn't seem real.

"Hey!"

I looked up at Megan.

"I said help me get him inside."

"He's alive?"

"There's a pulse."

I knelt down and helped her roll him onto his back. Once we had him turned over, I saw what was left of his face.

I'd heard about what frostbite could do, but I'd never seen it up close. Syl's face looked like someone had painted him with shoe polish. His nose was shrunken and black. His cheeks were swollen and the color of asphalt. The skin around his eyes looked waxy and there was a forest of white spots that ran down his neck then disappeared under his coat.

"Can you lift him?"

"I think so," I said. "If we can sit him up."

Megan grabbed his arms and pulled him into a sitting position. I knelt and started to drape him over my shoulder, then I saw Zack come around the corner. He was carrying his snow shovel and smoking a cigarette.

Megan waved him over.

Zack raised the cigarette to his lips then dropped it in the snow and started toward us. When he got closer and saw what we were doing, he tossed the shovel aside.

"Give me a hand?" My voice shook. "We need to get him inside."

Zack stopped behind me and stared at Syl.

He didn't move.

Megan told him we needed to hurry.

Zack muttered something then stepped closer and together we got him standing, each of us under an arm.

Megan ran through the snow toward the office.

We followed.

———

"Put him over there," Butch said. *"Next to the fireplace. I'll get* some blankets."

Zack and I eased him down to the floor then Megan moved in and started to unzip his coat.

"What are you doing?" Zack asked.

"His clothes are wet," Megan said. "We have to get them off and get him dry, or he'll freeze."

Caroline and Marcus were up and standing behind me, watching. "Where did he come from?"

I shook my head, didn't speak.

"Probably got caught in the storm and tried to walk," Megan said. "I can't believe he survived."

"Good Lord," Caroline said. "The poor man."

I stood and watched Megan pull Syl's clothes away from his skin, then I started inching my way toward the office door. I didn't know what I was going to do, but right then, every instinct I had was screaming at me to get out, to get back to the room and grab Sara and the suitcases and just run.

We could take our chances on the road.

I was still backing away when I looked up and saw Zack standing next to the fireplace, staring at me. Everyone else was completely focused on Syl, but Zack wasn't paying attention to anything but me.

I stopped backing up and looked at him.

He nodded.

Megan pulled off Syl's shirt then she leaned in and looked at the bandage. When she sat back she said, "That's a bullet wound. He's been shot."

There was a commotion, then everyone took a step closer and looked down at Syl. I turned and walked out of the room and into the office.

Butch was coming the other way. He was carrying a stack of yellow blankets and didn't see me.

"Sorry, Minnesota," he said. "Are you leaving?"

"I have to tell Sara what's going on." I motioned back to the dining room. "I guess that guy's been shot."

Butch's eyes went wide. "You're kidding?"

"That's what they're saying."

"Holy shit." Butch looked past me toward the dining room then held out the blankets. "Do me a favor and take these in there. I've got a first aid kit in the back, might help."

I didn't take them at first, but I didn't know how I could say no. "I need to get to Sara and—"

Butch pushed past me and ran out of the office.

I watched him go, then I carried the blankets into the dining room. Megan and Zack were kneeling over Syl. Caroline was arguing with Marcus. Zack was the only one who looked at me when I walked in.

No one else had noticed I'd left.

"What the hell do you mean there's nothing we can do?" Caroline was yelling at Marcus and the slur in her voice was worse. "We can't just sit here. Look at the man."

"Well, what do you suggest?" Marcus leaned back in his chair and motioned toward the window with his coffee cup. "The highway is closed. More than that, it's completely buried under snow. We'd drive off into a ditch within five miles."

I walked past them and set the blankets on the floor next to Megan. "Butch went to get a first aid kit," I said. "But he gave me these."

She took one of the blankets off the top then unfolded it. "Help me sit him up."

Zack reached down and grabbed Syl's shoulders and lifted him enough to get the blanket under him. Megan wrapped him tight then took another blanket and draped it over him.

"I'm not going to accept that," Caroline said. "If we don't get him to a hospital he's going to die."

I heard the bells over the office door then Butch came in carrying a large metal box. There was a red circle on the front with a white cross in the middle. He sat it on the table and undid the latches.

"No idea what's in here, but there might be something we can use." He looked at Syl. "How's he doing?"

"Unconscious," Megan said. "But breathing."

I got up and looked over Butch's shoulder at the first aid kit. All I saw were Band-Aids, individually packaged over-the-counter pain pills, and saline eyewash bottles.

"How old is this kit?" I asked.

"Old." Butch looked at me. "Does this stuff go bad?"

"I think we're beyond first aid," Caroline said. "He needs to get to a hospital or else he's going to die."

"Closest thing we've got to a hospital is forty miles north in Frieberg. I don't see how we can—"

"You've got a plow," Caroline said. "On that truck you used this morning in the parking lot. I heard it."

"It broke," Zack said. "I snapped the mounting pin."

"Can you fix it?"

"Even if it was brand-new, it wouldn't work on a highway, especially not all the way to Frieberg. That plow barely handled the two or three passes it took to clear the lot out there."

Caroline looked at Marcus then to Butch. "I think we have to try, don't you?"

"I just told you, the mounting pin is busted. We've got nothing to hold it in place."

"You can't find a way to rig it so it'll work?"

"Jesus, Caroline, the man just said—"

"How about that wire you got back there?" Butch asked.

Zack shook his head. "Too thin, won't work."

"You can try it, can't you?" Caroline said.

"I'm telling you that plow wasn't made to go long distances like that. It isn't going to work even if I do get it mounted and secure."

"And I'm telling you," Caroline said, "if this man stays here, he dies."

Zack stared at Caroline for a moment then he took a deep breath and ran his hand over his chin and said, "Maybe I need to talk slower."

Caroline looked at Butch. "Can you help me, please?"

Butch didn't say anything.

"Jesus Christ, doesn't anyone get it?" Caroline looked around the room. "This man is going to die."

"Zack," Butch said. "Why don't you try it. If it doesn't work, at least we made the effort."

Zack turned to Butch and whispered, "This is pointless and you know it."

"Just try it."

Zack stared at Butch then shook his head and pushed himself to his feet. He motioned toward me and said, "I'm going to need an extra pair of hands. You up for it?"

Everyone was looking at me.

There was no way to get out of it.

19

I followed Zack out of the office and across the parking lot. He walked fast and I could hear him mumbling to himself under his breath as we went. I did my best to keep up, but the muscles in my chest felt sore and cold, and I wanted to throw up.

When we got to the end of the building, Zack stopped and turned back. He took a few steps toward the office then stopped again, talking to himself, breathing steam into the air.

I waited for him and didn't say a word.

All I could think about was Sara and what I was going to say to her. My mouth tasted sour and I leaned over into the snow and coughed.

Nothing came up.

I stepped back and saw Zack reach up and run a hand through his hair then kick the snow hard and say, "Fuck." He spun around and walked past me toward his room.

I followed.

Once we turned the corner I told him I was going to check in on Sara. At first I didn't think he heard me, then he looked back over his shoulder and said, "I don't give a shit. It doesn't matter anyway, this isn't going to work."

I hoped he was right.

Zack stopped. "Who the hell is she to tell me? All of a sudden I'm her fucking servant? Do this, try that, fix this, make it work." He stood back and yelled toward the office, "If I say it ain't gonna work, then it ain't gonna fucking work, you cunt!"

I kept quiet.

When he finished, Zack took a deep breath and let it out slow, then he looked at me and said, "Sorry, Nate. I'm letting her get under my skin."

I thumbed back over my shoulder and said, "I'll catch up with you in a few minutes."

"Whatever, man, the truck is around back when you're ready. I don't care."

I turned and walked away.

When I got to our room, Zack was still standing in the middle of the parking lot staring toward the office. I thought about Butch telling me not to worry about him, that he just had a different way of looking at the world, but it didn't make me feel better.

I stood at the door for a while, going over everything in my mind. I knew I needed to tell Sara about Syl, but I had no idea how to do it.

There was really only one way.

———

"No." Sara shook her head. *"He's dead. You said he was dead."*

"I said I couldn't find a pulse, that's all. You're the one who said he was dead."

"He wasn't breathing, I swear." Sara brought her hands up and covered her mouth. "Nate, we left him out there, alive."

When I heard her say it out loud, I felt all the strength go out of my legs. I reached out and braced myself against the table then eased down to the chair.

I sat for a moment then leaned forward and rested my head in my hands. I didn't look up for a long time.

"What are we going to do?"

I could only think of one answer.

I stood up and grabbed my suitcase off the floor and set it on the bed. "Get everything together. I'm going to load the car."

Sara didn't move.

"We'll double-back to I-80. The roads can't be that bad, and the Dodge does good in the snow. I think it's worth a shot."

"What about the notebook? They know who we are."

I reached into my pocket and pulled out the page with our information and dropped it on the bed. "I got it."

Sara picked it up and turned it over in her hands.

"Hey," I said. "We've got to go."

"Nate, hold on."

I ignored her and reached for Syl's green backpack lying next to the bed. His clothes were still inside along with the sterile gauze and the twenty thousand dollars.

I thought about taking the money out and putting it in the suitcase with the rest, but I didn't want to take the time.

"Grab anything you unpacked."

"Nate, we can't leave."

"We don't have a choice." I picked up one of the suitcases then started for the door. "I'll be back for the rest, so hurry."

Sara got up then crossed the room toward me and took the suitcase out of my hand. "Just wait a minute."

"Sara?"

"We can't leave like this," she said. "Think about how it'll look." She took my hand and led me away from the door. "Just sit with me, let's think this through."

The last thing I wanted to do was sit down. Instead, I paced the room from one end to the other and tried to slow the thoughts screaming through my head.

"Go over it again," she said. "From the beginning."

So I did.

When I finished, Sara said, "He's that bad?"

"Worse."

"And they don't think he'll make it?"

I shook my head. I couldn't talk anymore.

Sara noticed, then reached out and took my hand. She pulled me over to the bed, and this time I sat next to her.

"We didn't know," she said. "This isn't our fault."

I looked at her, and the desire to tell her the truth was almost overpowering. If I'd had the words to explain why I did what I did, they would've come pouring out. I wouldn't have been able to stop them.

But there were no words.

"If we panic and try to leave now, everyone will know," she said. "We have to act calm and try to ride this out. Do you agree?"

I told her I did.

There were tears pressing behind my eyes, and I blinked hard to keep them back.

Sara leaned in and put her head against my shoulder. When she spoke next, her voice was a whisper.

"I love you, Nate."

I believed her.

Someone knocked on the door, soft.

I got up and reached for the gun on the nightstand, but Sara stopped me.

"Nate, no."

I hesitated, then set it down and walked to the door.

Zack was standing outside smoking a cigarette and kicking snow off his work boots. When I opened the door he looked up at me and smiled.

"Did you forget about me?"

Sara came up behind me and put her hand on my back.

When Zack saw her, he nodded and said, "Hello again. How are you feeling?"

"Fine." She looked at me. "Forget about what?"

"Hold on a minute," I said.

Zack motioned toward the office. "Did Nate tell you about all the excitement we've got going on today?"

Sara nodded.

"You know, I've seen some crazy stuff around here, but I've never seen anyone just come out of a storm like that guy did. After being shot, no less." He looked past us at my suitcase on the bed. "You two packing up?"

"Give me a second," I said. "I'll be right out."

"Sure, take your time." He held up his cigarette. "I'll be over by the truck when you're ready."

He turned away, and I closed the door.

"What's he talking about?"

I told her about the broken plow and about Caroline's plan to use it to try and get Syl to a doctor.

She frowned. "And you volunteered to help?"

"No," I said. "I didn't."

20

I walked around behind Zack's building and saw him standing next to a dirty white pickup truck. He had a cigarette in his mouth and a roll of bailing wire in his hand. When he saw me, he dropped the cigarette on the ground and let it smolder a moment before crushing it under his boot.

"Glad to see she's feeling better."

"Yeah, me, too."

Zack turned and opened the tailgate. The bed of the truck was coated with rust and lined with several fifty-pound bags of sand. There was a large red metal toolbox sitting against the side of the bed. Zack pulled it over and opened the latch.

He handed me the bailing wire and said, "Unroll about six feet. I'll try to find something else we can use."

"You don't think this'll work?"

"It'll prove we tried, but it won't work." He motioned toward the front of the pickup. "The mounting bracket snapped in half. Tell me what you think."

I walked around and saw the rusted metal bracket on the

front of the truck. It was still attached, but it'd been split along the base. Even if we could get the plow reattached, it wasn't going to hold.

Zack was right.

"I don't care how much wire we use," Zack said. "This truck ain't going all the way to Frieberg. We'll be lucky to get a mile or two down the road."

"How about without the plow?" I motioned to the sandbags in the back end. "What if we put more weight in the back?"

Zack didn't look up from the toolbox. "Not with those tires. Not a chance."

I stepped back and saw what he meant. The tires were worn to wire. I thought about asking how the truck moved in snow at all, but changed my mind.

I started to unroll the wire.

When Zack found what he was after, he closed the toolbox then slid it back against the side of the truck bed. He slammed the tailgate, but it wouldn't latch.

It took several tries to get it to close.

"How old is this truck?" I asked.

"Old," He said. "But it does the job. At least it used to."

Zack came around to the front of the truck and set a crusted tube of epoxy on the hood. He watched me unroll the wire for a while then said, "Why are you two packed?"

"We were going to try our luck on the road," I said. "Thought we'd look for a phone that worked and get an ambulance out here."

"What for?"

"What do you mean, what for?"

Zack looked at me like he didn't know what I was talking

about, then he said, "That guy in there is already dead. You know that as well as I do."

"We might be able to help him."

"Help him?" Zack laughed. "Now that's funny."

I kept quiet.

"Well, you do what you want," Zack said. "It might look better if you stick around, but I won't stop you."

"Look better?"

Zack smiled. "You figure it out."

I didn't need to. I understood.

"You know, I had a feeling you two were thinking about leaving." Zack took a piece of yellow paper out of his pocket and held it up for me to see. "So, I went ahead and wrote down your license plate number in case you got stuck and we needed to send the state patrol out to find you."

"You didn't need to do that," I said.

Zack put the paper back in his pocket. "I figured it was better to be safe. Weather around here can be unpredictable."

I started to say something else, but he cut me off.

"You and I really should bust the seal on that Johnny Walker bottle when we're done here," he said. "We have a few things to discuss."

"Like what?"

"We can start with you telling me what you were doing in my shed last night, and what you saw. After that, I'm pretty much open."

I started to explain about the unlocked shed door, but I stopped myself. I didn't see the point.

"I'll leave it up to you."

"I'm not much of a drinker," I said.

"One won't kill you."

"What if I say no?"

Zack looked at me for a moment, then he smiled and pointed to the roll of bailing wire in my hand.

"Six feet."

———

It took a while to get the plow attachment mounted, but eventually we did. Zack thought by threading the bailing wire through the mounting bracket then coating it with epoxy, no one would be able to say we didn't try. It looked good and it felt sturdy, and when we were finished, I had a sick feeling that it might actually hold.

Zack didn't.

"Time to show the queen in there that I was right."

"I don't know," I said. "It looks good to me."

Zack ignored me then walked around the truck to the driver's side and got in. When he started the engine, a thick black cloud of exhaust rose into the air. It hung for a moment before the wind carried it away.

"You want to come along?"

I told him I was going back to my room.

"Think about that drink," he said.

I told him I would.

Zack nodded then put the truck in gear and pulled around the building, kicking up snow as he went.

I watched him go, then followed.

When I got to the side of the building, I heard a loud screech and the sound of metal grinding on metal.

I ran around the corner and saw Zack getting out of the truck. The front mounting had snapped and the metal edge had ripped into the fender. The plow itself was caught under the wheels, and from where I was standing, one of the tires looked shredded.

Zack walked around front then knelt down and tried to work the plow loose. When it wouldn't come free, he got up and started pacing through the snow, talking to himself.

I watched him for a while, then I turned and went back to our room.

21

Sara was waiting for me on the bed when I went inside. I told her about the plow, then I told her Zack wanted to have a drink and talk.

"You don't drink anymore."

"I know that."

"What does he want to talk about?"

"He knows I was in his shed."

"That's it?"

"Far as I know."

"Then he didn't see you last night."

I wasn't convinced of that, so I didn't say anything.

Sara was quiet for a minute, then she said, "Did he really write down our license plate?"

I didn't actually see the numbers on the piece of paper, but it didn't matter. He knew something, and he was letting me know it. I told this to Sara.

"So, you're going over there?"

"I have to."

"He might be bluffing."

"Maybe," I said. "Or maybe not, I don't know."

Sara turned away and stared out the window, and for a while neither of us said anything.

I looked around the room.

There was a small writing table next to the window and a dresser against the far wall. I got up and pulled the dresser away from the wall and looked behind.

"What are you doing?"

"Looking for a place to hide the suitcase." I pushed the dresser back. "Just in case."

"What's wrong with under the bed?"

"It'll be the first place anyone looks," I said. "We have to put it someplace else."

"Who do you expect to come looking?"

I told her I didn't know, and I didn't.

It was just a feeling.

I checked the bathroom, but it was too small.

When I came out Sara said, "How about in the bed?"

"In the bed?"

She walked around to the headboard and grabbed the edge of the mattress then slid it to the side. "We can put it inside the box spring."

I stepped closer and pulled the mattress the rest of the way off then leaned it against the wall.

There was a thin fabric covering the box spring. I bent down and grabbed a corner and tore it away.

"All we have to do is bust a few of those wood slats and pull the springs out of the center," Sara said. "Then we put the suitcase inside and cover it with the mattress."

The wood slats were old and starting to rot. Breaking them wouldn't be a problem, but I thought the springs might be tough.

I told Sara to wait, then I grabbed my coat off the chair and went outside. I walked around the building toward the office.

Zack's truck was still sitting in the parking lot.

I stood out there for a while to make sure he wasn't around. When I didn't see him, I figured he'd gone inside to argue with Caroline.

That was fine with me.

I went around back and climbed over the tailgate into the bed of the truck then knelt in front of the red metal toolbox. I opened the latch. I didn't know what Zack kept inside, but I was sure I'd find something I could use.

I was right.

When I opened the lid, the first thing I saw was a black claw hammer. I grabbed it then shuffled around and found a heavy screwdriver. I set them both beside me then shut the toolbox and climbed out of the truck.

When I got back to the room I showed Sara the tools.

"Where did you get those?"

I told her and she frowned.

"I'll return them when we're finished," I said. "Unless you want to pull those springs out by hand."

She didn't say anything else.

We pulled the box spring off the frame and I used the hammer to bust out three of the wood slats in the middle. The springs underneath were rusted, and several of them came loose without a fight.

Others took some work, but eventually we'd cleared out enough space for the suitcase.

"Try it," I said.

We moved the box spring back to the frame then slid the suitcase into the center. It dropped in perfectly.

There was still some room along the sides, so we filled it with the broken wood and rusted springs. When we finished, we slid the mattress back in place.

No one would be able to tell.

Sara smiled. "I told you it'd work."

She was right, and I told her so.

Then I kissed her.

———

Once the room was clean, I grabbed the tools then went outside and walked down to the office. I stood against the building and smoked two cigarettes before I was sure no one was around, then I crossed into the parking lot and climbed into the back of the truck.

There were footprints around the toolbox.

For a second I felt my stomach twist, then I realized they were my footprints from before. I shook my head then opened the latch and put the tools back inside.

When I got back to the room I told Sara.

She didn't seem to care.

I asked her if she was okay.

She looked at me. "I think we should go see Syl."

"Why?"

"Because it'll look weird if we don't."

"I don't think you want to see him," I said. "He's in bad shape. You might—"

"I'll be fine."

She leaned over and grabbed her shoes off the floor and put them on, then she looked around for her coat.

I didn't move.

When she noticed, she said, "Come on, let's go."

"Are you sure you're okay?"

Sara made a dismissive sound, short and soft. "No, I'm not okay. Not at all."

"You still want to see him?"

"I can handle it."

Sara found her coat. She slid it over her shoulders then sat next to me on the bed. "Are you coming with me?"

I reached for her hand. She didn't want to give it to me at first, but in the end, she did.

"I'm sorry about this," I said. "I know this wasn't what you wanted, and I didn't think—"

She pulled her hand away and stood up. "That doesn't matter, not anymore."

"It does matter. I never would've—"

"Nate." Sara stopped me. "We've got two choices. We can come clean, or we can keep going and hope for the best."

"What do you want?"

She hesitated. "We're in too deep to come clean."

Hearing her say it thrilled me, and I couldn't help but smile. "Maybe we'll get lucky."

Sara looked away. "If we do, it'll be a first."

22

We left our room and crossed the parking lot toward the office. The sky outside had turned heavy and there was a cold wind coming in from the north. Thin wisps of snow spun around us as we walked. I tried to stay focused and tell Sara what to expect when she saw Syl, but all I could think of was the coming storm.

"You're worried about this, aren't you?"

I lied and told her I was fine.

"You think I won't be able to handle it."

"I just want you to be ready."

"I'm ready," she said. "Don't worry about me."

So, I didn't.

Zack's truck was still sitting out front when we got to the main building. We walked past it, then I opened the office door and motioned toward the dining room.

Sara went in first and I followed.

Megan was standing along the far wall, staring out the

window. Caroline was sitting on the floor next to the fireplace. She had a stack of paper in her hand.

They both turned when we walked in.

Caroline waved us over then pushed herself up.

As we got closer, I saw Syl lying in front of the fireplace, cocooned in several yellow blankets. His face, a polished purple, was the only part of him not covered.

He looked worse than I remembered.

When Sara saw him she stopped and made a short gasping sound. I reached for her hand, but she pulled away.

"I'm fine."

"Frostbite," Caroline said. "It does nasty things." She held her hand out to Sara and introduced herself. "I'm happy you're feeling better. I heard you had a bad night."

"Just a long one," Sara said. "Thanks."

Caroline introduced Megan then we all sat at the table next to the fireplace.

Caroline dropped the stack of papers on the table and said, "I was reading him some of Marcus's poems, but I don't think he can hear me."

"It can't hurt to try," Sara said.

Caroline smiled. "No, honey, it sure can't."

"Where is everyone?" I asked.

"Marcus is back at our room, sleeping, I'm sure. Butch and Zack are off somewhere, so it's just the two of us." Caroline paused. "Well, three of us."

"How's he doing?" I asked.

"He needs to get to a hospital," Caroline said. "But apparently that's not going to happen."

I ignored the angry tone in her voice and said, "Do you think he's going to die?"

"You'll have to ask her." Caroline pointed to Megan. "She's the doctor."

"Doctor?"

"Not a doctor," Megan said. "Just a student."

"He looks terrible."

Megan nodded. "If he does survive this, he'll probably lose his nose and several of his fingers." She looked at him and shook her head. "Caroline's right. We need to get him to a hospital."

"Any news on the snowplows?" I asked.

"We haven't heard anything."

I told them how the sky looked on our way over and that I thought another storm was on the way. They listened, and for a while no one said anything, then Megan took a cell phone out of her pocket and flipped it open.

"You have a phone?"

Megan nodded. "Don't get too excited. There's no signal out here. I've been trying all night, and now my battery is almost dead."

I wasn't sure if I felt relieved or not. I looked over at Sara. She was staring at Syl.

"You okay?" I asked.

"I didn't think he'd be this bad."

"He's also lost a lot of blood," Megan said. "Between that and spending the night in the storm, it's amazing he's alive." She flipped her phone closed and dropped it on the table. "Still no signal."

"Has he said anything?"

"Nothing that makes sense," Caroline said. "He mentioned something earlier about a woman named Lilith, but that was it."

"He'll wake up and say a few words then he'll drop out again," Megan said. "Actually, that's a good sign."

I felt my stomach cramp and I knew I had to get up. I stood and walked toward the fireplace and knelt next to Syl. His eyes were closed, and his skin was dotted with white blisters. I could hear the low rattle of his breathing. It sounded slow and thin.

I stayed there for a while, half listening to the conversation at the table behind me, then I saw Megan stand and come sit next to me. She put her fingers against his neck and didn't speak.

When she took them away I said, "Did you get a pulse?"

"Strong and steady," she said. "He's a tough one."

She unwrapped the blanket and looked at the bandage on his side. It was clean and new, but when she peeled back the corner, the skin underneath was black and smelled warm and fleshy, like rotted meat.

I made a noise and turned away.

"He's infecting," Megan said. "That's the problem. I don't think he has much time left."

I didn't say anything.

She replaced the bandage then looked at me and said, "Did you two see anything last night when you drove in?"

"Like what?"

"A car along the side of the road? Someone walking?"

"I barely saw this place," I said. "I almost drove past it."

Megan nodded then looked away.

Behind me, Caroline called my name.

I turned around.

"Are you much of a reader?"

"No," I said. "Not really."

She nodded, slow, like it wasn't a surprise. "I've been think-ing a lot about those old mystery novels. You probably don't know them, but they always start with a group of strangers thrown together around a dead body, usually in a secluded old mansion or on a remote island somewhere."

"Or in a motel during a blizzard," Megan said.

"That's right," Caroline said. "And I've been thinking about how strange it is to be in one of those situations in real life." She motioned to Syl. "Of course, we don't have a body, but we do have this poor man who we barely know anything about."

I didn't catch it at first, then I did.

"Barely know anything?" I asked. "We don't know anything about him, do we?"

Caroline pointed past me to a stack of mud-streaked clothes sitting on one of the tables.

"His wallet," she said. "There's not much to go on, but it cer-tainly raises some interesting questions. Have a look."

I got up and walked across the room toward Syl's clothes on the table. They were folded and stacked and still wet from the snow. Several lines of water ran off them and dripped onto the floor. Syl's money clip, thick with cash, was sitting next to a cheap metal watch and a black billfold.

I picked up the billfold and flipped it open to a laminated ID and a clean, gold badge.

For a second, I forgot to breathe.

The ID said his name was Sylvester White, and that he was a detective with the Chicago Police. The photo was an older one. It showed a younger Syl in uniform, straight and smiling against a pale blue wall.

I stared at it for a long time.

I heard Sara slide her chair away from the table and cross the room to where I was standing. I didn't want her to see the badge, but I didn't have a choice.

To her credit, she didn't react at all.

"So far," Caroline said, "we know he's from Chicago and he's a police detective and that someone out there shot him." She paused. "Everything else is a mystery."

23

Sara wanted to leave, so I said I'd meet her back at the room. Once she was gone, Caroline asked me if I would mind watching Syl for a couple hours later that night.

"We're all taking turns," she said. "Butch is coming back this afternoon, then Megan and Marcus are taking shifts tonight. We could use the help later this evening, if you don't mind. All you really have to do is make sure the fire doesn't die."

I told her I'd be happy to help.

Caroline smiled and touched my shoulder. "Thank you, Nate. Butch's nephew is staying overnight, so you won't have to be here for long."

"What happens if something happens?" I hesitated. "What if he dies? What are we going to do?"

"There's nothing we can do," Megan said. "Once the phones come back on, we'll call the police. Hopefully he'll make it that long and we can get him to a hospital."

"If he doesn't?"

"Then he doesn't." She looked at me. "All we can do is try

to keep him warm and comfortable. At this point, it's out of our hands."

Caroline made a dismissive sound.

I ignored her then looked down at Syl.

He shifted under the blankets then coughed and mumbled something I couldn't understand. Megan knelt on the floor next to him and whispered in his ear.

Whatever she said, it was too soft for me to hear.

"He's been doing this a lot," Caroline said. "He'll wake up and start mumbling about some Lilith woman, then he'll calm down and drift off again." She frowned. "It's very sad. I wonder if she's his wife."

"What does he say about her?"

"Hard to tell," she said. "Just her name, mostly."

I watched Megan sit back and grab the iron poker beside the mantle and use it to stir the logs in the fire.

Caroline looked at her and frowned. "Is that really necessary? It's already so hot in here."

"We need to keep it as warm as possible." Megan leaned the poker against the fireplace then came back to the table and sat down. "You get used to it after a while."

I thought I heard a trace of an accent in her voice.

"You're from Russia?" I asked.

Megan nodded then looked away. "St. Petersburg."

"Your accent," I said. "It's not there all the time."

"It comes out once in a while," she said. "But I work hard to hide it."

"Why?"

She seemed to think about it for a moment, then she said, "I would like to put Russia behind me."

"How do you get rid of an accent?" Caroline asked.

"You sing," Megan said. "I used to spend hours singing along to American songs. You don't have an accent when you sing. That's how actors do it."

"Well, it obviously works," Caroline said. "You sound like you were born and raised right here."

Megan smiled. "Not quite, but thank you."

They talked for a while longer, and I did my best to listen, but I kept staring at the jagged scars on Megan's arms. I wanted to know what they were from, but I couldn't bring myself to ask.

Eventually, Megan noticed and pulled her sleeves down over her wrists. "It's not what it looks like."

"I'm sorry," I said. "I didn't mean to—"

"It's okay."

I paused. "You didn't like Russia?"

She looked at me and I thought she was trying to smile. If she was, it didn't work.

"I'm happy to be here," she said.

I decided to let it go.

After a while I pushed back from the table and stood up. "I should check on Sara."

"Of course," Caroline said. "We'll see you tonight, and thank you for agreeing to help. Maybe the phones will come on or the plows will come, and we won't need you."

"I hope so."

"Just keep your fingers crossed."

They already were.

I stood outside the office and stared north toward the playground and the single cottonwood tree in the distance. I wasn't in a hurry to get back and face Sara, so I took a cigarette from my pocket and lit it.

I'd smoked half of it before heading back to the room.

When I opened the door, Sara was kneeling over her suitcase. The others were packed and sitting next to the bed.

I stood in the doorway, watching her.

"This is the last one," she said, not looking up. "But you have to figure out what to do with that stuff." She pointed to the gun and the backpack on the nightstand. "I'm not touching those."

"I'll take care of them," I said.

She sat back on her feet, examining the suitcase, then looked up at me and said, "Are you going to take the bags?"

"Now?"

"Yeah, now," she said. "I want to leave."

I didn't move.

"Nate, come on."

"We can't leave right now," I said.

"You said the Dodge would do good in the snow."

"What about Zack?"

"What about him?"

"He'll know why we left. He'll tell the police."

"Let him." She closed the bag then got up and lifted it off the bed and set it next to the others. "We've got money. We can go anywhere in the world, right?"

I nodded.

"So let's go someplace they'll never find us."

"Where?"

"I don't care," she said. "As long as it's far away."

I stepped toward her but she backed up.

"You know where I always wanted to go?" She didn't wait for my answer. "Brazil. That's far away, isn't it?"

I told her it was.

"It's hot down there," she said. "You'll like that."

"Sara?"

"Did you know they have their own Mardi Gras? They call it Carnival. I watched a show about it one time. They have big parades and everything."

"We can't leave," I said. "Not yet."

She looked at me. "He's a cop, Nate."

I nodded.

"And he's alive."

"I know."

"How is that possible? Did you see his face?"

I told her I did, then said, "I don't think he's going to last much longer."

"What if you're wrong? What if he lives? He's going to be like that for the rest of his life, and we'll go to prison. I don't want to have this baby in jail, Nate."

I didn't know what to say, so I kept quiet.

After a while, Sara said, "Can I ask you something?"

"What?"

"Promise me you'll tell me the truth, okay?"

I promised.

Sara looked at me. "Did you know?"

"That he was a cop?" I shook my head. "How could I have known that?"

"No," she said. "Did you know last night? Did you know he was still alive when you went out there?"

I didn't answer right away, and something changed in Sara's eyes.

She tried again.

"When you took him into the field. Did you know?"

"No." I hesitated. "Not at first."

"Not at first?"

"When I was leaving," I said. "I thought I heard something, but I wasn't sure. My head was—"

"You didn't go check?"

"What was I going to do, carry him all the way back? You saw me last night. I barely made it on my own."

Sara stared at me. "You left him out there."

I didn't say anything.

"Why didn't you tell me?"

"And say what? We both thought he was dead. What was I supposed to do?"

Sara backed away from me, then turned and went into the bathroom and closed the door. I heard the lock click shut. I went to the door and listened.

She was crying.

"I didn't know what to do," I said.

No answer.

"I did what I thought was best for you and the baby. I didn't think he'd make it." I felt a cold ache at the base of my skull and I tried to ignore it. "You weren't there, Sara. I'm the one who had to make the decision. What the hell did you do?"

I kicked the door, hard, then backed away and paced the room. My hands were shaking, but I barely noticed. I tried to think about what to do next, but the pain in my head was getting worse and nothing came to me.

I needed to get away until I calmed down.

I went to my suitcase and took out my pills and popped two of them into my mouth and swallowed them, then I put the bottle back. I sat for a while then I stood up and grabbed Syl's backpack off the floor.

"You want to leave? Fine, we'll leave."

I slipped the strap over my shoulder then picked up one of Sara's suitcases and walked out into the parking lot. When I got to the car, I opened the door and tossed the backpack and Sara's suitcase into the backseat, then I changed my mind.

I didn't want Syl's backpack in the car.

Having his suitcase was dangerous enough. It didn't seem smart to drive around with a bag full of his clothes, which might link us back to him. All we needed from the backpack was the twenty thousand.

Everything else of his could go.

Except the gun.

Sara wasn't going to be happy about that, but as long as we had the money, I was keeping the gun.

I'd get rid of it once we got to Reno.

I reached in and grabbed the backpack off the backseat When I did, I saw Zack step out of his room and onto the porch. He saw me then waved and started walking down the steps toward the car.

"Fuck."

I bent down and shoved the backpack as far under the driver's seat as it would go, then I stepped back and closed the door.

When Zack got close, I said, "How's your truck?"

He shook his head. "That was a disaster, wasn't it? I wanted to prove her wrong, but not like that. Looks like I've got to come up with the cash for a new tire."

"Sorry to hear it."

"You know, I needed new ones anyway. This was just God telling me to get moving on it." He pointed to the car. "What's this?"

"I'm loading the car."

He looked at me. "You decided to leave after all?"

"Just getting ready."

"I see," he said. "I hope you stay long enough to have that drink. What about later tonight?"

I told him I'd agreed to watch Syl.

Zack shook his head. "The queen's idea, am I right?"

I told him he was.

"That woman." He shook his head. "Well, how about now? You can grab your girlfriend and finish this later."

I opened my mouth to tell him no, then I thought about him writing down our license plate number, and I knew I'd have to talk to him eventually. With Sara locking herself in the bathroom, I figured now was as good a time as any.

It'd been years, but right then, a drink sounded pretty damn good.

"Give me a minute," I said. "I'll head over."

— — —

When I went back inside, Sara was still in the bathroom. I knocked on the door and said, "I'll be back in a while."

At first, nothing, then I heard the lock slide away.

The door opened a few inches.

"Where are you going?"

"To talk to Zack. I want to get this over with, find out what he knows." I paused. "Sara, I really thought I was doing the right thing for you and the baby, for us. I didn't think—"

She slammed the bathroom door and locked it.

I stood for a moment and stared at the closed door. I could feel the muscles in my chest get tight, and I fought the urge to say something else. I knew if I did, I'd never be able to take it back, so I kept quiet.

On my way out, I went to the nightstand and picked up Syl's gun. I checked the clip and the safety and thought about taking it along. In the end, I decided not to.

I set the gun back on the nightstand and walked out.

24

I stood outside Zack's room until I'd finished my cigarette, then I knocked twice and waited. When he opened the door, he looked at me like I was the last person he expected to see.

"Hey, Nate." He looked past me. "Where's your lady? She didn't come?"

"Was she supposed to?"

"Just thought she might." He stepped back and held the door. "Come on in."

I stepped inside.

The layout of the room was the same as ours except for a utility kitchen against one wall and a long couch under the window. There was an ebony crucifix hanging over the bed, and a poster of an aborted fetus above the television with the words "Why, Mommy?" printed in large white letters along the bottom.

"I don't drink much these days," Zack said. "But with all the excitement around here, I thought it would be a good idea if you and I got to know each other a bit." He went to the counter and held up a bottle of Johnny Walker. "I can't tell you how long this has been sitting around gathering dust."

I stared at the poster and didn't say a word.

He poured the whiskey into two glasses then came up and stood next to me. When he saw me looking at the poster he said, "What do you think of that one?"

"It's subtle."

Zack laughed, quick and short, then held out one of the glasses. "Subtlety has no place against the wicked, Nate, remember that."

I took the glass and sipped. The whiskey filled my sinuses and scorched my throat when I swallowed. I hadn't had a drink in years, and it took a while until the burn passed. When I was sure my voice wouldn't crack, I said, "So, what's all this about?"

Zack smiled, showing his teeth. "Don't be in such a rush. Neither of us got anyplace to be, am I right?"

I was still on edge because of Sara and I wanted to argue, but I didn't. Like it or not, he was holding all the cards, and it wouldn't do me any good to get on his bad side.

Zack crossed the room to the couch and sat down. "How long were you in prison?"

I looked at him, didn't speak.

"Your girl mentioned it when we talked this morning. I hope that's okay."

It wasn't okay, not at all.

"She said you killed a kid, is that true?"

I took a drink and tried to stay calm. "My brother," I said. "He was fifteen. It was an accident."

"How do you accidentally kill someone?"

"It was a car accident," I said. "I was running from the cops and lost control. He was thrown."

"That's tough."

I didn't say anything.

"Why were you running?"

"I had guns in the trunk," I said. "Lots of them."

"That's what you went to jail for?"

"You've got a lot of questions," I said. "Is this what you want to talk about? Prison?"

"In a way, I suppose it is," Zack said. "I did ten years up at Anamosa. Worst time of my life in some ways, but the best in others."

"Yeah, what'd you do?"

"I shot a guy who owed me money." Zack took a drink and winced. "Wow, that's a bite."

"Did he die?"

"No," Zack said, drawing the word out. "Came close, but he's still out in the wild with the rest of the herd."

We were both quiet for a while, then I said, "If you think we're going to bond over prison, you might be disappointed. I did most of my time in the infirmary."

"Because of—" He motioned to my head.

I nodded.

"What happened?"

"Some kid wanted to make a name for himself. I was new, so I was a target."

"What'd he do?"

"Took a weight bar from the yard then came up behind me and called my name. When I turned, he was already halfway through a full swing. I don't remember any of it."

"That's a blessing."

"If you say so."

"Looks like they pieced you back together okay," Zack said. "Hell of a scar."

"Got a plastic plate the size of a baseball in there, and sometimes things get all swimmy on me. The headaches are the worst, but I can live with them."

"Headaches?"

I nodded.

"Bad ones?"

"Yeah," I said. "Bad ones."

"How long were you inside?"

"About a month in the general, fourteen in the infirmary," I said. "Eight of those I spent in a coma, so it went by quick."

"All by the grace of God."

I pulled a chair away from the table then sat down and took another drink. This time it didn't burn as much. It almost tasted good. I set the glass next to a stack of pro-life pamphlets. They were blue with heavy ink, Bible verses, homemade.

"You're pretty serious about this abortion stuff, aren't you?"

Zack smiled. He set his glass on the nightstand next to the couch then leaned forward and braced his elbows against his knees. "Tell me something, Nate. Will you?"

I told him I would.

"How much do you know about our Lord and Savior?"

"As in Jesus?"

"That's right."

"Just what I picked up in Sunday school."

"How much was that?"

"Enough," I said.

Zack nodded. "Most people feel the same way. I was one of them. I'd heard the stories and thought I had it all figured out, but I was dead wrong, believe me."

"Let me guess. You found God in prison."

Zack laughed. "You can try to minimize it all you want. You can write me off as just another person who hit rock bottom and had no way to crawl but toward the Bible, and that's fine. Most people do. But it's not the truth."

"What's the truth?"

"I didn't find God in prison," he said. "God found me in prison. You know where?"

I shook my head.

"Sitting in the corner of my cell covered in my own shit and piss, sweating and puking from all the dope I'd been on when I was out in the streets." He paused. "Do you know what he said to me?"

"God spoke to you?"

"He said I'd been chosen. He said the beasts were at the door, and from then on it was up to me to hold His ground." Zack sat back, chin high, eyes focused. "He said from then on, I was to be a warrior in His name."

Zack stared at me for a long time.

Neither of us spoke.

"I know you were in my shed, Nate."

I didn't deny it.

"You know what's in there, don't you?"

I told him I did.

Zack took a drink. "Proverbs, twenty-one, two. Do you know it?"

I shook my head.

"'Every man is right in his own eyes, but the Lord ponders the heart.'"

"I don't understand."

"It's a war, Nate. It's a war against the swine infesting God's creation." He motioned to the pamphlets. "You ask me if I'm serious about the infanticide happening every day in every city around this country? I tell you, it's the fucking front line of it all."

I kept quiet.

Zack watched me. "Which is why I wanted to talk to you." He sat back. "See, I was debating how to handle you snooping around out there, but then—"

"First off, I wasn't snooping. The wind blew the door open and I was trying to do you a favor."

Zack held up his hand. "Let me finish."

I did.

"See, I was debating. Should I let it go, or should I chop you up and throw you in a freezer until the snow cleared and I could get you down to the Cormans' pig farm."

I smiled.

Zack didn't.

"So, I asked God for guidance and He told me to go down and talk to you. At first it seemed pointless, but I went." He tapped his finger at me. "And here's where God worked His magic. You weren't around, but your girl was, and when I found out she was pregnant, I knew you'd understand my situation."

"What situation is that?"

"The war," he said. "It's not cheap. We can't afford to lose ground and let ourselves slip into the gutter with the filth. If that means taking money from drug addicts who are doomed to hell anyway, then that's what I'm going to do." He paused. "That's what you found out in the shed. You found my investment."

"What does Butch think of it?"

Zack waved a hand in the air, dismissing me. "Butch is going to hell in his own way. He doesn't pay attention to anything I do around here."

I waited, then said, "You were a drug addict."

"That's true."

"Are you damned to hell like the others?"

Zack laughed. "No, I've proven myself to God."

"But being around drugs, that's got to be a temptation. You don't think God doubts your will?"

Zack reached for his glass on the nightstand and said, "God doesn't doubt my will."

"You sound serious."

"He doesn't doubt my will."

I didn't say anything.

Zack watched me. "In prison, after I got through my withdrawals, I knew I had to prove to God that my will was strong enough to handle what He was asking of me."

"How'd you do that?"

"The covenant of the flesh."

I shook my head, shrugged.

"It's not something discussed in Sunday school?"

"I guess not."

Zack nodded. "Circumcision."

"As in—"

"As in, I took the blade from a disposable razor and stood over the sink in the back of my cell and proved my will to God."

I was quiet for a long time, then said, "Jesus."

Zack took a drink. "God doesn't doubt my will."

I had no idea what to say, so I kept quiet.

"I hope you understand about the shed and what you saw. I want you to see the greater purpose."

"Your secret is safe."

Zack smiled. "You know, I was doubtful about you at first, but as usual, God was right."

"Then you don't need our license plate number."

"No use for it, as long as we're on the same page."

I told him we were.

Zack reached into his breast pocket and took out the slip of paper and handed it to me. "Then here you go."

I turned it over in my hands.

It was blank.

Zack laughed. "Got your attention, didn't I?"

I faked a smile then dropped the paper on the table and said, "You sure did."

"Thought I would."

I drank the last of my drink then started to stand. "I should go, but thanks for the drink."

Zack didn't move.

"Good luck with the war."

"Thank you."

I pushed myself up and moved toward the door.

Zack stopped me.

"One more thing, Nate. If you got a minute?"

I felt something heavy settle at the base of my spine.

"Our friend in the office? The snowman?"

"What about him?"

"You know I watched you carry him into the field last night, don't you?"

I didn't speak.

Zack waited, then said, "I'd love to know why."

25

"Were you the one who shot him?"

"No," I said. "All we did was give him a ride."

"Then who did it?"

"No idea."

Zack leaned back on the couch and stretched his arms out over the cushions. He asked me to go over everything again, so I did. I told him about the diner and the bathroom and the ride through the storm. I told him about seeing the motel then finding Syl dead in the car.

"But he wasn't dead," Zack said.

"Obviously not."

Zack stared at me. "Go on."

I told him everything I could remember, and I tried to stick to the truth. Except when it came to the money.

That, I lied about.

"Two hundred thousand dollars?" Zack opened his eyes wide and exhaled sharp. "That's a lot of cash."

"Yeah," I said. "It is."

"Where's it now?"

"We've got it."

Zack got up and grabbed the bottle off the kitchen counter. He refilled my glass then his. "You really thought he was dead?"

"I checked his pulse and couldn't find one."

Zack took a drink then sat back on the couch. "So, you figured you could ditch the body out in the field, then when the roads were clear you'd disappear with the money and no one would know any different?"

"Pretty much."

"But then the guy pops back up like a bad penny."

I wanted to ask if he was the one who dragged him out of the ravine, but I wasn't sure I wanted to know. Instead, I said, "It wasn't what I was expecting."

"I bet it wasn't." He swirled his drink in the glass. "Two hundred thousand is a good start for a new family."

"It sure is."

"So, now what?"

I thought about it for a second then said, "I don't know. I guess it depends on him."

"If he lives or not."

"That's right."

"What if he dies?"

"Then we stick to the plan," I said. "If he doesn't die, then I don't know what we're going to do."

"You two are in a bad spot."

I agreed, then said, "What would you do?"

"For two hundred grand I'd do a hell of a lot." Zack leaned his head back and looked up at the ceiling. "You know he's probably not going to die. He should, but he's a tough son of a bitch."

"You're right about that."

"We can speed things along."

I looked at him, didn't speak.

"I'm watching him overnight. I can make sure he doesn't make it until morning."

"Kill him?"

Zack shrugged. "I'll use a pillow. No one will know. It'll look like he died in his sleep. No one will think anything of it. Simple."

"Why would you do that?"

Zack smiled. "Money."

I hesitated. "How much?"

Zack sat up and finished his drink in two large swallows. "What if I wanted it all?"

"Then you and I would have a problem."

Zack smiled. "Yeah, I suppose we would."

"Try again."

He sat back and looked past me at nothing, then said, "A hundred thousand seems fair. Even split. Half for me, half for you two."

"That's still a lot."

"It'll solve your problem."

"And fund the war?"

Zack nodded. "And fund the war."

I thought about it for a second. "I'd have to talk to Sara."

"Whatever you have to do," Zack said. "You can come back with the money when you decide." He motioned to the bottle. "You want another drink for the road?"

I told him I didn't.

Zack shrugged then poured himself one.

I got up and grabbed my coat. "I'll come back and give you an answer."

Zack followed me to the door.

I opened it and stepped out into the snow.

"It's all in how you sell it," Zack said. "If your girl doesn't like the idea, tell her you don't have a choice. I'm sure she'll understand."

"We always have a choice," I said.

Zack smiled and closed the door.

———

I took a cigarette out of my pocket and lit it then stepped down into the parking lot. The sky was turning dark, and a wall of bruise-colored clouds hung just above the horizon. Any hope I'd had about the storm missing us disappeared.

It was coming.

I put the cigarette to my lips and inhaled, deep. I could still taste the whiskey in the back of my throat, and I turned and spit into the snow.

It wouldn't go away.

When I got to our room, I stayed outside and leaned against the building and finished my cigarette.

I thought about Vincent.

It'd been a long time since I'd talked about him to anyone, and I didn't like it. Whenever I did, the memories came flooding back and they wouldn't go away.

I didn't need that now.

I looked down at my feet and felt a sharp flash of pain in the middle of my head. I closed my eyes and tried to push it away. I didn't want to think of anything but what I needed to do for Sara and the baby.

I told myself that when all this was over I'd sit and think about Vincent. I'd make sure I remembered everything I could about him. The sound of his voice, the way he laughed, the look on his face when he was happy.

I'd bring it all back.

But not now.

Not yet.

Right now, I had to stay focused.

When I opened my eyes again, everything was fine.

———

When I got back to the room, Sara was sitting up in bed folding clothes into one of her suitcases. When she saw me, she almost smiled.

"You're out of the bathroom," I said.

"Since we're not leaving, I figured I could pack these a little better."

I sat next to her. "Can we talk?"

She didn't look up.

"I can't keep saying I'm sorry."

She ignored me, said, "How'd it go?"

I didn't know what to say.

It would've been easy to tell her that Zack agreed to keep quiet for a price. Then, when Syl died overnight, she wouldn't know the difference. It would've been easier, but I wasn't going to do it. I didn't want to lie anymore.

So I told her the truth.

She didn't say anything, just cried for a long time.

I tried to tell her it was the only option and that we had to see the plan through to the end.

"This was never the plan."

"I know," I said. "But it's too late to go back."

She looked at me but didn't say anything. There was nothing to say. It really was too late to go back. Our only chance was to pay Zack and hope for the best.

We got up and I pulled the mattress off the bed. I opened Syl's suitcase and counted out the cash, then looked around for something to put it in. While I was looking, I noticed the Bible sitting out on the nightstand. I figured Sara must've taken it out of the drawer. I started to ask her about it, then changed my mind. It was her business.

I took one of the pillows off the bed and stripped the case, then I dropped the money inside.

"What if he finds out?"

"Finds out about what?"

"About the money," Sara said. "What if he finds out how much is really here?"

"He's not going to find out," I said. "We're the only ones who know, and we're not going to tell him."

"I don't like this, Nate."

"Yeah," I said. "Neither do I."

26

I knocked on Zack's door and heard him shuffling inside. I waited, then knocked again.

"Who is it?"

I told him.

The door opened less than an inch. He looked out at me, then disappeared. A moment later the door swung open.

"What are you doing here?"

I held up the pillowcase.

He looked at it then at me. "Is that it?"

"That's it."

He moved out of the doorway and I went inside.

The smell, chemical clean and poison sweet, made my eyes water. I was about to say something, then I saw the carbon-stained glass pipe on the nightstand by the bed, and I knew for sure what was going on.

"I thought you said—"

I stopped myself.

Zack had lied to me, but it didn't matter. As long as he did his part tonight, I didn't care what else he did. There was no point in creating more tension.

Zack was staring at the pillowcase. His eyes were dilated solid black and there were thin beaded lines of sweat on his skin.

"You okay?" I asked. "Are you still up for this?"

"Let me see the money," Zack said. "Show me."

I handed him the pillowcase. He sat on the bed and didn't say anything for a while, then he reached in and took out one of the wrapped bundles of cash and fanned his thumb over the edge of the bills.

"Damn, you weren't lying."

"Did you think I was?"

Zack shook his head. "No, I had faith in you, Nate."

He turned the bag over and dumped the money out on the bed then laughed, quiet.

"I wouldn't mind another drink," I said.

"Help yourself."

I got up and walked over to the utility kitchen and found the glass I'd used earlier. I rinsed it out at the sink then looked around for the bottle.

"I don't see it."

"Cabinet."

I opened the cabinet then grabbed the bottle and filled my glass halfway. It was more than I needed, but it'd been a tiring twenty-four hours.

I came back and sat on the chair by the table and watched Zack pick up each bundle and run his fingers over the bills. He was smiling. His teeth looked like charcoal candy corn.

"Tonight, right?"

Zack looked up. "What about it."

"Syl," I said. "Tonight."

At first, it didn't seem to register, then his eyes cleared and he said, "Our snowman, right." He turned back to the bills. "I didn't know that was his name."

I was pretty sure I'd told him Syl's name when I'd gone over what'd happened, but maybe I was wrong.

I lifted the glass and took a drink, then said, "Tell me something?"

"What's that?"

"Were you the one who pulled him out of the ravine?"

Zack looked up at me. A second later he smiled then said, "Yes and no."

"What does that mean?"

"It means I didn't pull him out of the ravine, but I did drag him out of the field." Zack looked back at the money and started stacking the bills. "I waited until the storm broke then wandered out to see what you were up to. I found him about a hundred yards in. It looked like he'd gone most of the way himself before he dropped."

"Why leave him? Why not take him inside?"

"Then what?" Zack shook his head. "I probably should've left him where I found him, but I didn't, and it wasn't until I got almost all the way back that I started having second thoughts." He looked at me. "But, what's done is done. Now we move on."

He was right.

I didn't like it, but he was right.

I took another drink then said, "How are you going to do it?"

Zack opened the pillowcase and started putting the money back inside.

"Zack?"

"Yeah," he said. "I'm thinking."

I let him think, then when he had the money put away I said, "We should figure this out."

"I haven't decided."

"I think you should."

He ignored me. "Something not obvious by looking at him. At least not right away." He shrugged. "I don't know, Nate, but God will show me what path to take."

"What about the pillow? Isn't that what you said?"

He looked at me and smiled. "You don't need to worry. When you wake up in the morning, it'll be over."

"I hope you're right."

"I am right," Zack said. "It's as good as done."

———

Sara and I spent the rest of the afternoon in our room. We packed all the bags and I set them next to the door. Then we waited.

I spent most of the time at the window, staring out at the parking lot and the fields in the distance. The snow was falling again, but not like the night before. This time it came slow, delicate, like an easy dream.

Any other time and it would've been beautiful.

"What are you looking for?" Sara asked.

There was a dead fly lying on its back in the windowsill. I stared at it for a moment then let the curtain close.

"Nate?"

"I'm not sure," I said. "The plows, I guess."

"You'll hear them when they come."

"I want to be prepared."

Sara didn't say anything else.

I sat at the table and time passed.

"Do you think Zack's really going to do it?"

I told her he was.

"How can you be sure?"

"Because of the way he looked when he saw that money," I said. "He's not going to turn it over to the police."

"What if he doesn't follow through? Then what?"

"He'll follow through."

"But what if he doesn't?"

"You're borrowing trouble."

"No, I'm not."

"You're thinking of all the bad things that can happen and you're focusing on them. It's not helping."

Sara was silent. She didn't move.

I watched her out of the corner of my eye, hoping for something, but she just stared at me. When I couldn't take it anymore, I looked at her and said, "What?"

There were tears on her cheeks.

I moved to the bed and held her until she stopped shaking, then I said, "We're going to be fine."

"None of this is turning out how I thought it would."

"It can still work," I said.

Sara nodded.

"What's wrong?"

"Nothing."

I told her I didn't believe her.

"You'll just get mad."

"It depends on what you say."

"The money," she said. "I don't want it anymore."

"What?"

"Things are different now," she said. "Before we thought he was sick and that he just died. Somehow that seemed okay. Now, with Zack involved, we're going to be murderers."

I started to deny it, but for some reason, hearing her say it like that made it real. Even though we weren't going to be the ones who actually killed him, we were going to be just as guilty.

"You want to back out."

"It's not too late."

"Yes, it is."

"We can give the suitcase to Zack, or dump it somewhere for someone else to find."

"Sara—"

"It doesn't matter what we do with it," she said. "Once it's gone, we can pretend none of this ever happened. We can go back to our old life."

"No, we can't," I said. "I can't."

"Why not?"

"Because there's nothing there to go back to."

Sara stared at me, silent.

"What do you think I'm going to be able to do for us, or for the baby?" I ran my hand over the scar on the side of my head. "I can't get a decent job with my record. We'll never have money."

"That doesn't matter."

"It matters to me." I paused. "What kind of father do you think I'm going to be?"

"You'll be a great father."

"I wasn't to Vincent," I said. "Look at the job I did with him."

"You weren't his father."

"I was the closest thing he had to one."

"Nate, don't do this, please—"

"We can use this money to start off right. It might be my only chance to do something good for this kid." I looked away. "Without it, there's nothing."

"There's us."

"Not enough."

She watched me for a long time without saying anything, then she moved close and kissed me, soft and slow. "Do you love me?"

I told her I did.

"Then we'll be fine."

We stayed like that for a while, then she added, "And you're going to be a great father."

It was what she was supposed to say, and even though I didn't agree, I didn't argue. She loved me too much to see it any other way, and I knew enough not to try and convince her otherwise.

She'd figure it out eventually.

When it came to love, everyone always did.

27

I was back at the window watching the snow gather in the parking lot and thinking about Zack. Sara was sitting on the bed. She'd found a deck of cards and was practicing dealing blackjack, preparing for the future.

It was a good sign.

"I can't be in here anymore." Sara stacked the cards then set them on the nightstand. "I'm losing my mind. I have to get out of here."

"The roads are still—"

"This room, Nate. I have to get out of this room." She walked to the table and grabbed her jacket. "I need to eat something. I feel like I'm going to pass out."

"Where are you going?"

"To the office. They might have something there."

"But—"

"I'll be fine," she said. "I know what I'm doing."

I got up and reached for my coat.

"You don't have to come," she said. "I'll be fine."

But I went anyway.

I thought the fresh air might do us good.

———

Sara saw her first.

The woman was standing alone at the edge of the playground and staring out at the field and the single cottonwood in the distance.

"Who is that?"

I stopped walking and looked back. When I saw her, I felt my stomach twist. For an instant, I couldn't speak.

"Nate, who is—"

"I don't know," I said.

We stood and watched her, then she turned and walked toward the right side of the playground.

"It's Caroline," I said.

"What is she doing?"

My heart was beating double time, and all I could do was shake my head.

"Do you think she's okay?" Sara asked. "Does she need help?"

"She's fine," I said. "Let's go."

I turned and kept walking toward the office.

Sara followed.

It was unsettling to see Caroline out there, standing in that spot. It was too familiar, too coincidental, and something about it burned in the back of my mind.

I told myself she was tired of being inside, just like us, and she needed to get out and walk, even if it was through the snow.

It sounded possible and I mentioned it to Sara, even though I didn't believe it myself.

She didn't believe it either, and by the time we got to the office, I could tell she was starting to worry.

"What was she doing out there?"

"Walking."

"But why that spot?"

"You're doing it again." I did my best to sound calm. "Let it go."

Sara frowned, but she stopped talking.

I opened the door and we stepped inside.

The air in the office was hot, and I could hear Syl moaning in the other room. We followed the sound.

"Where is everyone?"

The room was empty except for Syl on the floor by the fireplace. He was twitching under the blanket like a giant yellow worm. As I got closer, I saw that the skin on his face had dried and begun to peel away in thin, dead gray strips.

"Who's supposed to be in here?" Sara asked. "What happens if he wakes up and needs something?"

I looked at her. She seemed to realize what she was saying and she turned away.

"Are you sure you can handle this?"

She nodded.

"Why don't you wait in the other room. I'll look for something to eat."

"No."

"It might be easier."

"Let's just grab something and go."

We looked around, but we didn't find much.

There were individual packets of oyster crackers on the counter and some instant oatmeal. We put the crackers in our pockets and left the oatmeal behind.

"I wish there was fruit around here," Sara said. "I'd kill for an apple."

Behind us, Syl coughed then said, "No, I don't know."

We both turned around.

Syl's eyes were closed.

A second later he coughed again, then he was silent.

Sara didn't look away from him until I reached out and touched her arm.

"Come on," I said. "Let's go back."

"We should stay until someone shows up."

"Sara."

"It'll make me feel better."

So we did.

A few minutes later we heard the bells above the office door, then Marcus came into the dining room.

When he saw us, he stopped. "Hello, Nate."

I motioned to Sara and introduced her.

"Caroline's husband," I said.

Marcus had a hardcover book under his arm. He set it on a table then unzipped his coat. "Pleased to meet you."

"We didn't think anyone was in here," Sara said.

"I ran back for my book." Marcus pointed at Syl. "Our friend here isn't much of a conversationalist. Megan was here for a while. Did you see her on your way over?"

"We saw Caroline," I said.

Marcus frowned. "Yes, I know. Was Butch with her?"

"I didn't see him," I said. "Is she okay?"

"Bored. At least I hope that's what it is. She's taking all of this rather seriously."

"All of what?"

"This," Marcus said. "Our friend over there." He paused. "She can't seem to come to terms with the fact that we're stuck out here, and now she's acting like Miss Marple, out trying to solve a quaint Midwestern murder."

"He's not dead," Sara said.

"That's right." Marcus pointed a finger at her. "You and I can see that, but for some reason it's lost on her. And now with someone going around breaking into people's rooms, Butch is all worked up, too. They're a regular Holmes and Watson."

"Someone's room got broken into?"

Marcus tapped his finger against his chest. "Just my room and Butch's place. Nothing was taken, but things were thrown around." He pointed toward the door. "If you ask me, it's his own damn nephew doing it. That kid isn't right."

"Why is Caroline outside?"

"No idea," Marcus said. "She insists she knows what's going on. Didn't say what she knows or how she found out, but she seems serious. It's damn silly, if you ask me."

I felt Sara tense up next to me.

I pretended not to notice.

"It's easy to let your imagination run wild out here," I said. "Especially in this situation."

"Caroline doesn't need much help in that regard."

"At least she's keeping herself busy."

Marcus pointed toward Syl. "He's been talking a lot more.

It's all nonsense to me, but maybe he said something to her that clicked."

"She didn't tell you anything at all?" Sara asked.

"Not a word," Marcus said. "When I showed up, she just grabbed her coat and ran out. And to be honest, I've learned not to ask. I know there's no talking to her when she's like that."

Sara and I looked at each other.

Marcus sighed then picked up his book and sat at the table by the fireplace. "Sometimes, I just don't get that woman." He shook his head. "Damn silly."

28

We carried the food back to our room then locked the door behind us. The first thing I did was slide the mattress off the bed and check the suitcase.

It was still there.

"What are you doing?" Sara asked.

"Making sure no one's been in here."

Sara leaned against the wall then opened a package of crackers and ate them one at a time. She didn't look at me, and neither of us said a word.

I pushed the mattress back in place.

Outside, the wind was picking up, and occasionally it would slam against the building and rattle the windows. Every time it did, Sara would jump. When I noticed her hands shaking, I figured I should say something.

"Don't be upset," I said. "Everything's going to work out. Caroline doesn't know anything."

"I don't want to talk about it."

"You're worried."

"Doesn't mean I want to discuss it."

I watched her for a while then got up and grabbed my coat off the chair.

"Where are you going?"

"Outside."

"What for?"

I took my cigarettes from my pocket and showed her.

She stared at them then turned back to her crackers.

"What do you want me to say?"

"There's nothing to say," she said. "Things are the way they are. It's too late to say anything."

"You said we could ride this out."

"I know what I said."

"We can still do it."

"Do you think so?"

"You don't?"

"I think this isn't going to end well," Sara said. "Not as long as we have that money."

"What the hell does that mean?"

"That money is cursed."

My first instinct was to yell at her.

The flash of anger was so strong and came so fast that it shocked me into silence, and that was a good thing.

I turned and unlocked the door.

"Hold on," Sara said. "Don't go yet."

"I'm not getting rid of the money."

"Nate, I—"

I told her again, louder this time.

"I'm not getting rid of the money."

Sara looked at me. "We could lose everything."

"We don't have anything."

"We have each other," she said. "And we have the baby. That's all that matters."

I didn't speak.

"Jesus, Nate, you could go back to prison."

"I'm not going back to prison."

"You could if Zack goes through with—"

"I'm not going back to prison, no matter what."

Sara looked like she had more to say, but instead she got up and came to me and buried her head against my chest and stayed like that for a long time.

Eventually, she pulled back and looked up at me.

"All I want is you. Do you know that?"

I told her I did.

"The money isn't important unless I have you."

"Not right now," I said. "But in a few years, when you've had me around for a while, you'll think it's important and you'll wonder about what could've been."

She looked up at me and smiled, but it never touched her eyes. "You don't know me at all, do you?"

———

I leaned against the side of the building and smoked my cigarette. The snow was falling hard, and heavy gray clouds settled low over everything.

Somewhere in the distance, I heard a door shut.

I went to the end of the walkway and looked out at the office. Caroline and Butch were walking up the path toward our building. I wasn't surprised to see them.

I watched until they got close then I dropped my cigarette in the snow and waited.

"Nate," Caroline said. "You got a minute?"

I told her I did, then added, "How's the detective work coming?"

She didn't understand.

I explained my conversation with Marcus.

Caroline frowned. "I'm glad he sees the humor in all of this, and you, too."

I told her it was a joke and tried to laugh it off, but she didn't care. I invited them inside, out of the cold.

"This won't take long," she said. "We can talk out here."

I took another cigarette from my pocket then lit it and said, "It's up to you."

Butch was staring at my lighter, frowning.

I remembered the matches and said, "Found it in my bag. I didn't need those matches after all."

Caroline looked at Butch then back at me. "You were the last to arrive last night, right?"

"I don't know about that, but we got in late, sure."

"Do you remember seeing any other cars on the road?"

I told her I didn't.

"How about anyone walking?"

"Megan already asked me all this," I said. "You want to know if I saw him out in the storm."

Caroline waited for me to answer.

"If I'd seen him, I would've picked him up."

"So, you didn't."

"No," I said. "I didn't see anyone."

Caroline looked at Butch and something unsaid passed between them.

"Why are you asking me?"

"We're asking everyone," Butch said. "Not just you."

"But you're suspicious of me."

"We've had some problems around here today," Caroline said. "And I'm afraid your name keeps coming up."

"I'm not the one going through people's rooms," I said. "I've been inside with Sara all day."

"Marcus told you about that, too?"

I told her he had, then looked at Butch and said, "He thinks it's your nephew. Did you start with him?"

Butch shook his head. "It's not Zack."

"And it's not just the rooms, Nate," Caroline said. "Butch told me he caught you behind the front desk this morning. Now he's missing all your personal information from last night when you checked in."

"I don't know anything about that."

The both stared at me, then Caroline said, "And then there's the man dying back there in the office."

I waited.

"He knows your name. Can you explain why?"

I shook my head. "I helped carry him inside. Maybe he heard my name and remembered it."

"I don't think so."

"Why not?"

"He's been saying a lot more," Caroline said. "He mentioned money and a woman named Lilith. Do you know anything about that?"

"I don't know anything about any of this," I said. "What exactly are you accusing me of doing?"

"We're not accusing you of anything," Butch said.

"Then maybe it's a good idea if we stop talking before you do." I took one last drag off my cigarette then tossed it into the snow. "I'm heading over to the office in a little while to take my turn, unless you don't want my help anymore."

Caroline looked at me and I saw her eyes soften. "I don't know, Nate. Maybe I am taking all of this too seriously. If so, then I apologize."

Butch started to say something but didn't.

"I'll come by the office later and we'll play some cards," Caroline said. "We'll see if you're as bad as you say you are."

I lied and told her I'd like that, then I turned back toward my room.

Butch stopped me.

"I need to get all your information again." He reached into his pocket and took out the notebook. "Before you leave."

"I'll give it to you when I get over to the office," I said. "I want to get back inside before Sara starts wondering what happened to me."

I could tell Butch didn't like the idea, but he didn't say anything. Instead, they told me to say hello to Sara then they turned and started back toward the office.

I didn't stick around to watch them go.

29

I didn't say anything to Sara when I went inside, and she didn't say anything to me until she saw me take the gun out of the nightstand drawer and check the clip.

"What are you doing?"

"Being safe," I said.

"Nate, I don't think—"

"I'm not asking for your opinion."

She didn't say anything else.

I slid the gun under the back of my belt then went into the bathroom and ran the water hot in the sink. My face felt numb from the cold, and the water stung when it touched my skin. But it cleared my head.

Things were falling apart, and I could feel myself slipping. Even if Syl died tonight, there would still be questions, and all eyes would be on me.

The pain behind my eyes was strong.

I turned off the water and went out into the room. My pills were on the nightstand next to the Bible. I opened the bottle and tapped three into my palm and swallowed them dry, then I motioned to the Bible and said, "What's with this?"

Sara looked then shook her head and said, "Nothing."

"Why do you have it out?"

"I don't know. It helps, I guess."

"You're going to wind up just like your mother."

Sara was quiet for a moment, then she said, "Do you believe in God, Nate?"

"I don't know what I believe."

"We've never talked about it."

"We've got bigger things to worry about now."

Sara looked at me and frowned. "You're mad at me, aren't you?"

"No."

"About the money," she said. "You are, I can tell."

"Not now, Sara."

"Are you still going to let Zack do this?"

"It's not my choice," I said. "He's involved now, and he's going to do it whether I want him to or not."

Sara looked down. "I can't believe this."

Part of me wanted to laugh and part of me wanted to scream at her. There was a voice in the back of my mind asking me what I'd expected from her, that she was just a kid and all of this was my fault for listening to her.

If we'd never given him a ride, none of this would've happened. If it was anyone's fault, it was mine for not being man enough to say no.

I pushed the voice away then slipped my coat on and opened the door.

"Nate, wait, please."

I stopped and looked back.

She opened her mouth to speak but nothing came out.

"I'll be careful," I said.

Sara nodded, and I walked out.

———

"She came to see you, didn't she?" Marcus asked.

I told him she did.

"And she got to you, too. I can tell." He laughed then placed his bookmark between the open pages of his book and closed it on the table. "Don't let her ruffle you. It's just the way she is."

"What way is that?"

"She's a bully, or didn't you notice?"

"Hard not to notice."

Marcus smiled. "She's like that with everyone. Ask our mailman or the guy who comes over and fixes our pipes. Hell, ask anyone she comes in contact with. The woman is a bully, plain and simple."

"I'll keep that in mind." I motioned toward Syl. "How's he doing? Still talking?"

"Not a peep," Marcus said. "Between you and me, I don't think he's going to last the night."

"That's too bad."

"Is it?" Marcus shook his head. "Look at the guy. I wouldn't want to live like that, would you?"

I stepped closer to Syl and saw the puffed skin and black blisters covering his face. I turned away and said, "No, I guess not."

Marcus and I talked for bit longer, then he put his coat on

and stuck his book under his arm and said, "I'm going to get some sleep. Sorry again about Caroline."

I told him it was fine.

"Be happy you get to drive away from her," he said. "Think about my life."

We both laughed, then he waved back over his shoulder and walked out of the dining room and into the office. A second later, the bells over the front door chimed.

I was alone with Syl.

———

I sat for a long time and listened to the wind press against the side of the building. When the fire started to burn down, I got up and grabbed another log off the pile then used the poker to open the spark screen. I set the log on top of the coals, and a few minutes later the fire was burning strong.

I looked down at Syl and heard a slow rattle of breath in his chest. He didn't move.

I thought about what Marcus had said about Syl not making it through the night. If he was right then Zack wouldn't have to do anything. We could wait it out.

The problem was getting Zack to agree.

I could talk to him, but I didn't think he'd listen.

And what if Syl didn't die? He'd already survived the storm and a gunshot. What if he survived this, too?

In the end, I decided it was better to be safe and let Zack handle it. I thought it would be better for everyone, including Syl. All I had to do was stay out of the way.

I walked back to the table and reached for Caroline's cards.

I took them out and shuffled them then laid out a game of solitaire. For a while, it took my mind off everything, and that was good. Zack wasn't coming for a few more hours, so I had time to think. If I got lucky, Syl would give up and go quietly in his sleep before Zack arrived.

If I got lucky.

I put a black queen on a red king then moved a red eight to a black nine. I felt good, but in the end I lost the game. I played again, but lost that one, too.

Eventually, I got tired and I put the cards away then leaned back in the chair and closed my eyes.

I don't know how long I was like that, but when I opened them again, the room was completely dark except for a carpet of red coals smoldering in the fireplace.

I got up and grabbed a couple logs off the pile then dropped them both on the coals. When I turned and reached for the poker, I noticed Syl was sitting up.

I made a sharp sound in the back of my throat and jumped away. I stood for a moment, staring at him, then the wood popped in the fireplace and caught fire, spilling a dancing yellow light into the room.

Syl's blanket had fallen off his chest and settled around his waist. I could see the bandage on his side, as well as several scars along his shoulders and chest. Some were thicker and longer than others, but each one looked bad, painful-bad.

I stepped closer.

Syl had his hands out in front of him, and he was staring down at his black fingers. He didn't seem to notice me.

I reached for a bottle of water on the table and unscrewed the cap and held it out to him.

He looked up, saw me, saw the water.

I moved it toward his mouth and helped him drink.

He took two swallows and coughed, heavy and deep. Blood flew from his mouth and covered my hand and ran down his chin. When he finished coughing, I held the bottle out to him again, but he shook his head.

I set it on the table.

He went back to staring at his hands, and he didn't speak for a long time. When he finally did, he looked up at me and said, "Where is she?"

His voice was thin, broken.

I noticed I'd been holding my breath.

I let it out, said, "Who?"

"Lilith," he said. "Where is she?"

"She's not here," I said. "It's okay."

Syl ignored me then looked past me toward the door. "She's here, I saw her here. Standing in the dark."

He was shaking, and I reached out and touched his shoulder. At first I didn't think he was going to calm down, but after a while I started to feel the tension ease away and his breathing slow.

"How are you feeling?"

Syl lowered his head and a long trail of saliva dropped into his lap.

"Do you need anything?" I asked.

Syl held up his hands. "What's this?"

I looked closer and saw Syl's hands in the firelight.

All the fingers on his right hand had been twisted and snapped at the middle knuckle, and each of them bent out at a different angle.

For a second, I couldn't find my voice.

I tried to remember if his fingers had been broken when we'd brought him inside, but I didn't know for sure.

I remembered watching Megan take off his clothes and wrap him in the blankets, but not his fingers.

I told myself Megan would've noticed, and she would've said something. But she hadn't.

Someone had gotten to him.

Which meant someone knew.

I sat back and tried to stay calm.

I wasn't ready to believe it, and I did my best to convince myself that he'd broken them coming out of the field, and I'd just overlooked it. It was the only explanation I'd accept, and after a while I started to believe it was true.

Syl asked again what had happened.

I leaned forward and told him about the frostbite, but I could tell it wasn't registering.

When I finished, he asked again.

He was in shock.

I told him again.

There were several long gray strips of skin hanging from his cheeks and wavering in the air like cobwebs. I tried not to look at them.

I told him about the storm and about the motel.

As I talked, Syl kept looking at his hands, turning them over. Every time he took a breath, his chest buzzed like a chorus of flies.

When I finished, we were both quiet for a long time. I watched Syl sway gently in front of the fire. I thought about asking him if he wanted more water.

Instead, I said, "Can you hear me?"

Syl let his hands drop to his lap, then he looked up at me. In the firelight, the whites of his eyes looked deep red, as if filled with blood.

"Yeah, kid," he said. "I can hear you."

30

"I don't blame you," Syl said. "But this is a hell of a way to wind up."

"Syl, what happened to your fingers?"

He looked at me like he didn't understand then down at his hands and said, "She did."

"Who?"

"Lilith," he said. "She wanted the money."

I looked away. "And what did you tell her?"

"I don't remember."

I frowned. He was obviously delirious, and there was no point in trying to get an answer. With Syl, everything seemed to circle back around to Lilith.

Syl coughed and a thick trail of blood came out of his nose and ran over his lips and dripped onto the blanket.

He didn't seem to notice.

"You know you won't be able to keep it."

"Why not?"

The look that crossed his face was probably a smile, but it was hard to tell.

"She's not going to let you."

"Who's 'she'?"

"Lilith."

"Even if she is out there, she won't find us."

Syl coughed again, and this time there was laughter behind it. "This is why I don't blame you."

I shook my head.

"You don't believe me?"

I told him I didn't.

"It's true, I don't blame you. I feel sorry for you, both of you, but I don't blame you."

"Sorry for us?"

"Neither of you have any idea what's coming."

"What's coming?"

Syl's eyes dipped shut for a second, and I reached out and touched his shoulder. He jerked back, his eyes opened.

"What's this about?" I asked.

"The money," he said. "She's following the money."

"Lilith?"

"We had everything planned. Her husband, she knew his schedule. She told me when he was home and when he'd be alone. I trusted her."

"Syl, I—"

"She told him she was out of town, but before she left, she unlocked a window. All I had to do was get inside and wait. The rest was easy."

"Did you kill someone?"

"He was a criminal," Syl said. "A wannabe gangster. It

wasn't a loss." He paused. "But I didn't do it for the money. I did it for her."

Syl looked up and I saw his eyes roll back. I thought for a second that he was going to pass out again, but he didn't.

"She was supposed to meet me," Syl said. "That's what we decided. Make it look like a robbery. Get in, pull the trigger, grab the money, then get the fuck out."

"She didn't meet you?"

"She was there."

I hesitated. "I don't understand."

"She was there, in the house. She was waiting for me." Syl looked at me. "She used me to kill her husband."

"Did she shoot you?"

"I grabbed the money and ran," he said. "I panicked."

Syl's body shook, but his voice was steady.

"She worked for him," Syl said. "Before she married him. I should've seen through it. I knew what kind of woman she was."

I didn't know what to say.

"I left town and took back roads, but it didn't matter. She knew what I'd do, who I'd call."

"You're a cop. You could've called other cops."

"No," he said. "I couldn't."

I waited for him to go on. Instead, he swayed slightly and his eyes fluttered.

He was fading. I needed him awake, so I kept talking. "She can't know you're out here."

"She knows," Syl said. "She knows because I fucked up." He coughed. More blood. "I called my brother. He kept a house out here somewhere for hunting. He was going to pick me up at that diner."

"Where we met?"

"When he didn't show, I called him again. Except this time she answered. She'd made him tell her where I was and where I was heading, then she killed him."

"Do you think she's coming?"

"She's already here," Syl said. "I've seen her."

"In the dark?"

"That's right."

I shook my head. "She's not here, Syl."

"You can't keep the money," he said. "She won't—"

He coughed again, and when he finished I saw him start to fall backward. I reached out and helped ease him back onto the floor, then I covered him with the blanket.

"Bring it here, leave it, then go."

I didn't say anything.

"Use your head, kid. It's probably too late, but if she gets the money she might just leave."

"We can run."

"She'll find you."

"How? We can go anywhere."

"She'll find you," he said. "And you don't want her to. She's got a black soul."

I sat back and stared into the fire. I was having a hard time taking any of this seriously. I couldn't help but think he was delirious or just making the story up to scare me into returning the money.

It wasn't going to work.

I started to ask him more about Lilith, but it wasn't any use. He was out again.

———

The fire had burned down, so I stacked a couple more logs on the coals then pushed them around with the poker until they caught.

I looked at my watch.

It was ten past midnight.

Zack was late.

I sat at the table and waited. Syl was where I'd left him on the floor. He hadn't moved or made a sound for over two hours, and the idea that I was the last person he'd ever talk to was up front in my mind.

That, and his story.

I wasn't sure how much I could believe and how much was delirium. Someone had shot him, and maybe he was telling the truth. Maybe he'd gotten involved with the wrong woman. It was possible, but to believe she was following him to kill him and take back the money?

That, I had a hard time believing.

I played the story over in my mind. It helped keep my thoughts quiet and off Zack and what was going to happen.

The only sound I heard was the occasional spark popping in the fireplace, and the tired moan of the wind outside. I kept expecting to feel that familiar sharp pain behind my eyes, but it never came.

No pain, just calmness and peace.

It didn't seem right.

With everything that'd happened, the last thing I should've felt was peace. But I did, and I didn't question it. Instead, I leaned back and put my feet up on the table and closed my eyes and thought about Sara.

I'm not sure how long I stayed that way, but when I opened my eyes again, I wasn't alone.

Caroline was standing across from me, pulling her gloves off one finger at a time. Butch was behind her, standing in the doorway.

They both stared at me.

"Sorry to wake you," Caroline said. "But I think we need to talk."

31

Now, the pain was there.

I sat up and rubbed the spot between my eyes with my fingertips then looked back toward the office. It wasn't bad yet, just a dull ache building in the center of my head. I cursed myself for leaving my pills in the room.

"I thought the bells would wake me up if anyone came in," I said. "I must've really been out."

"You were."

Caroline stacked her gloves then dropped them on the table and sat down. "How's he doing?"

"Woke up around ten," I said. "Nothing since."

"Did he say anything?"

"A little," I said. "A woman and some money."

Caroline nodded.

"You don't seem surprised," I said.

"It sounds like what I heard this afternoon."

"Did he tell you who shot him?"

"He told me a lot of things," Caroline said. "Which just led to more questions. That's why I thought we should talk."

"I still don't know how he knew my name."

"Not about that."

"Then what?"

"About your plans, Nate. You and Sara." She leaned forward and rested her elbows on the table. "This situation has her scared. You know that, don't you?"

"How do you—"

"Oh, I talked to her," Caroline said. "While you were sleeping." She smiled. "Actually, I've talked to everyone here. We all know what you two did."

"What we did?" I tried to smile, to look amused, but it wouldn't come. "You've got it all wrong."

"I don't think I do."

"Do you think I shot him?"

Caroline nodded. "That's one theory."

"Then you've got it all wrong. It's not true."

"People do a lot of things for money," she said. "And two million dollars is a lot of money."

I looked at her then opened my mouth to say something, but she held up one hand, stopping me.

"Don't bother to deny it," she said. "Sara confirmed the amount."

"The hell she did."

"Not in so many words, you're right, but you don't always need words." She tapped one finger under her eye. "Sometimes, all you need to know is right here. Windows of the soul, or so they say."

"You're lying."

"Nate, the poor girl is scared to death. She's practically crying out for help. All I had to do was provide a shoulder and she opened right up." She frowned. "You put her in a terrible position, and you don't see it."

I got up and grabbed my jacket.

"Where are you going?"

"Back to my room," I said. "Talk to Sara."

"She's fine," Caroline said. "Megan is with her."

"Why is Megan with her?"

"To keep her company. The poor girl is a bundle of shattered nerves right now, and the two of them seem to get along well. I swear she's fine."

I slid my coat over my shoulders and started for the office. Butch stepped into the doorway and didn't move.

I prepared myself to go through him.

"Nate, hold on," Caroline said. "Let's just talk before you go storming off and making things worse. Can we do that, please?"

I looked back at her. "If you talked to Sara, then she told you I didn't shoot him."

"That's what she told me."

"But you don't believe her either?"

"I'm not saying I don't believe her, or you," Caroline said. "I just want to talk."

"About what?"

She motioned toward the chair. "Sit, please. Five minutes, I promise."

I looked back at Butch then moved toward the chair and sat down.

Caroline leaned across the table. "I want you to know that I believe you. I don't think you shot anyone. You don't seem like that kind of person."

I nodded, but I wasn't sure I agreed.

I didn't know what kind of person I was anymore.

"I just want to know what happened," she said. "All I can do is piece together what I've heard from him, and it's hard to tell what's real and what's not, considering his state of mind."

I kept quiet.

Caroline looked at me, waiting for me to speak. When I didn't, she said, "You two do know each other, right?"

"What did Sara tell you?"

Caroline leaned back in the chair. "Give and take? Is that what this is?"

"I don't have to talk to you at all."

"No, but you will," she said. "You will because you're a good person at heart who made a mistake, and you're going to need someone on your side when the police get involved."

"I didn't shoot him."

Caroline paused. "I believe you."

Behind me, I heard the office door open. We all looked as Zack came inside.

Right away I knew something was wrong.

Zack's skin was pale and drenched with sweat. His eyes were the size of silver dollars and they jittered black in his skull. There were scratch marks on his neck, and when he walked, he seemed to stumble over his feet.

When he saw us, he stopped in the doorway and took off his jacket. "What's all this?"

Butch pointed at me. "This is the guy who shot our friend over there."

Zack looked at me and nodded. "That so?"

Caroline held up her hand. "We don't know that. All we're doing is talking. I'm sure it'll all make sense."

"I didn't shoot anyone," I said.

Butch leaned close to Zack and said, "Guy was carrying two million dollars on him. This kid took it."

If he'd been trying to whisper, he failed at it.

I closed my eyes, and when I opened them again, Zack was staring at me. I could see his jaw muscles pulse and twitch under his skin. At first I tried to tell myself that it was the meth making him grind his teeth, but I knew better. This wasn't the drugs.

This was rage.

The look in his eyes gave it away.

32

"Butch," Caroline said. "You're not helping."

"Just filling in the blanks."

For a while, everyone was quiet.

I could feel Zack staring at the back of my head, but I didn't turn around. Instead, I stayed focused on Caroline and tried to ignore him.

"Two million dollars," Caroline said. "You can see why people might think you were involved."

"Not if they knew me."

"But shooting a man for that kind of money isn't all that far-fetched. Even I'd be tempted."

Zack walked around the table and grabbed a log off the stack by the fireplace, then used it to open the spark screen. "She's got a point. Two million is a hell of a lot different than, say, two hundred thousand." He shook his head. "That's more than I've ever seen."

He smiled at me.

I ignored him.

"Sara told us you have a gun," Caroline said. "Is that true?"

"It's his gun, not mine."

"Can I see it?"

"No."

"Why not?"

"Because who the hell are you?"

"Nate, I—"

"You're accusing me of something I didn't do."

"No one is accusing anyone of anything."

"You're trying to muscle a confession out of me."

"You admitted you knew him."

"Not like you think."

"But you were involved, weren't you?" She hesitated. "Come on, Nate, we're all going to find out eventually."

I started to argue, but there was no point. She was right. Everyone was going to find out.

"You want to know the truth?"

I saw Zack turn, fast. He stared at me.

Caroline nodded.

I didn't say anything right away. I wanted to be sure I was doing the right thing. I figured I'd be telling the story to the police eventually, so I might as well tell her. At least then, I could get it off my chest.

So I did.

When I finished, Caroline frowned. "You thought he was dead?"

"We both did."

Behind me I heard Butch laugh. The sound was low and rolling. "My God, boy. You must've shit yourself when you saw him lying out there in the snow."

"Is there more?" Caroline asked.

I told her there wasn't, at least not that I knew about. Then I said, "I didn't shoot him."

"I believe you, but I'd still like to know who did."

I pointed at Syl. "He told me a woman named Lilith shot him. Said they'd planned to kill her husband and run off with his money."

"He told you that?"

I nodded. "He said after he shot the guy she turned on him."

"Sounds like bullshit to me," Butch said.

"The man's been through a lot," Caroline said. "It's hard to know what's true and what's a delusion."

"What did he tell you?" I asked.

"Nothing that made sense," she said. "He thought he was in Chicago, for one. He was frantic over this Lilith person chasing him, and about you stealing his money. He wasn't conscious for very long."

"That's it?"

"Honestly, I was so surprised when he knew your name that I didn't focus on much else. And like I said, he didn't make a lot of sense."

I thought about what she told me and tried not to let my imagination run wild. Still, something didn't feel right.

I turned to Butch. "Who was the last person to check in last night?"

"You were."

"No, there was a car after us. I saw it."

He thought about it for a moment then said, "I guess I can double-check. I put the notebook in my room to keep it safe, in case anyone else decided to rip out a few pages." He paused to look at me. "I'll be back in a minute."

Butch turned and walked out.

"What are you thinking?" Caroline asked.

I shook my head, didn't answer.

Zack started whistling a song I didn't recognize.

I looked up at Caroline.

She was staring at me, and the warm light from the fireplace reflected white off her glasses.

"Have you thought about what to do next?"

"I don't think I have many choices," I said.

"You should know that no one here blames you for what you did." Caroline reached for the deck of cards on the table. "I meant it when I said I would've been tempted, too. I think we all would've been."

"It's a lot of money to let go."

She split the cards and started shuffling. "Just bad luck on your part, if you ask me."

"I doubt the police are going to agree with you."

"Oh, they won't." Caroline dealt five cards facedown between us. "Then again, maybe they don't have to know."

I stared at her.

"Check your cards."

"I don't think I'm in the mood," I said.

Caroline ignored me.

"The trick to poker isn't playing the cards, it's playing your opponent. They'll tell you what they're holding if you know how to look. Do you understand?"

I hesitated then picked up my cards and fanned them out. I was two cards off a low straight.

"Luck doesn't play as big a roll in this game as people think." She pointed to my hand. "How many?"

I pulled two cards and pushed them across the table.

Caroline took two off the top of the deck and slid them over.

I missed my straight.

I wasn't surprised.

"All you have to know is how the person across from you plays the game. Once you do, you can use it to your advantage."

"What did you mean, the police might not have to know?"

Caroline didn't look up from her cards. "There are seven of us out here, right?"

I nodded.

"How much is two million divided by seven?"

Behind her, Zack stopped whistling.

Caroline looked at me. "Butch and I discussed it on our way over. We thought you'd agree that walking away with something is better than nothing."

"You want to split the money between all of us?"

"Why not?" Caroline sat back in her chair. "We'll all be equal partners, everyone comes out ahead."

"And Butch agrees?"

"He does," Caroline said. "So does Marcus, once I tell him. And Sara doesn't want the money at all, but I'm sure she'll do whatever you ask her to do. That little girl is crazy about you, Nate."

"What about Megan?"

"We'll talk to Megan."

"And him?" I motioned toward Syl. "What's going to happen to him?"

"That's Butch's area," she said. "Apparently he knows some-one who can help."

I looked past Caroline to Zack. He was standing next to the fire, staring at me. His face hidden in shadows.

Caroline turned her cards over on the table.

Three queens.

"Do we have a deal?"

I smiled, couldn't help it.

She asked again, and this time I answered.

"Yeah," I said. "We have a deal."

33

Zack went out for more firewood while Caroline and I stayed at the table playing cards.

I wasn't winning, but I was getting better.

I listened to her talk about Marcus and how they'd lost their entire savings in the stock market. I didn't follow the technical stuff, but it was clear that they needed money.

This was a good situation for everyone.

I'd just lost another hand when the chimes over the door rang and Zack walked in carrying an armload of wood. He was sweating and his breath was fast and heavy.

"I thought you might be Butch," Caroline said. "I wonder what's taking him so long."

"Maybe someone stole the notebook," I said.

Caroline laughed. "At least this time you have an alibi." She looked over at Zack. "Did you see Butch?"

Zack ignored her and began stacking the wood on the ground next to the fireplace.

Caroline waited then turned back to me and rolled her

eyes. "Well, he'll show up eventually, I suppose. Why did you want to find out who checked in after you, anyway?"

I motioned toward Syl. "The story he told me," I said. "And because of his fingers."

"His fingers?"

"They're broken. At first I thought it might've happened outside, but someone would've noticed when we brought him in."

"You think someone around here broke his fingers?"

I pictured someone leaning over him, snapping one finger after another, asking one question over and over.

Where's the money . . .

I pushed the thought away then said, "It's stupid, I know."

"It's not stupid," Caroline said. "I just wonder why anyone would do such a thing."

"If they knew he had the money and wanted to find it."

"Lilith?"

I shrugged. "Told you it was stupid."

I looked over at Zack. He was adjusting the logs in the fireplace with his hands. Reaching in, moving one, then pulling away fast, cursing under his breath, not paying attention.

"Everyone here knows about the money," Caroline said. "So, if Lilith is here, we'll never find out."

"That's why I wanted to see who got here after us. If she was chasing him, she would've come later."

"Well, I personally think he's delirious," Caroline said. "But if she is real, I hope she can live with a seven-way split."

We both laughed.

Zack stood and took the poker from beside the fireplace and used it to close the spark screen. "That should burn for a while."

"I don't see the point of keeping it so damn hot in here," Caroline said. "Do you?"

"I think it feels okay," I said.

"If you say so," Caroline said. "I'm warm-blooded, so I guess I'm always hot."

I looked up at Zack and saw him take a step back from the table. He stood for a moment, then lifted the poker over his shoulder and swung down hard, connecting with the top of Caroline's skull.

The sound, thick and wet, hung in the air.

Caroline made a sudden small choking noise deep in her throat then her eyes went wide and rolled over white.

Somewhere in the back of my mind, I thought I heard a voice, far away and thin. It sounded like laughter.

Zack pulled back on the poker, but the curved metal barb on the end had embedded itself in the top of her skull and wouldn't come loose. Each time he tried to work it free, Caroline's body would puppet back and forth, dancing jaggedly in her seat.

Finally, he put one foot on her back and pulled, ripping the poker out. The sound was like splitting wood.

Caroline fell forward.

Her head struck the tabletop and a swell of blood poured across the surface toward me.

I got up fast and backed away until I hit the wall.

"Give me the gun."

I was staring at Caroline, unable to look away.

Her body shuddered and twitched.

"Nate, give me the gun."

I heard the voice again.

This time it was close, and it was screaming.

"Goddamn it, Nate, give me the fucking gun!"

I looked up at Zack. He had the poker in one hand and was reaching out to me with the other.

I tried to speak.

Nothing came out but a moan.

Zack said something under his breath then turned toward Caroline. He raised the poker over his head and brought it down on the back of her skull, again and again, creating a fountain of blood and bone.

I felt my legs give out and I slid down the wall to the floor. The screaming in my head stopped and was replaced by blinding sharp pain.

I closed my eyes. When I opened them again, Zack was standing over Caroline's body, breathing hard. His face was freckled with blood and his eyes looked black and lifeless in the firelight.

When he saw me, he came at me fast. He grabbed the front of my jacket and pulled me to my feet then punched me hard in the stomach.

I felt the air rush out of my lungs and I dropped.

"You just can't do things the easy way, can you?"

I wanted to answer, but there was no air and no voice.

He picked me up again.

This time he pressed the end of the poker into my neck, just under my throat. I saw thick clumps of skin and bloody gray hair on the metal.

"What gives you the right to make that kind of deal without me? I'm supposed to be your fucking partner. What the hell were you thinking making that kind of split?" Zack motioned toward Caroline's body. "That is your fault. She's dead because of you, asshole, one hundred percent."

I closed my eyes.

Zack leaned in close, and I could feel his breath against my face. It smelled wet and ripe.

"Now," he said, slow. "Give me the fucking gun."

I hesitated, then reached behind my back and took the gun out of my belt and handed it over.

Zack let go of me.

"Is it loaded?"

I told him it was.

He looked at it for a moment, then walked back to the fireplace and leaned the poker against the wall. "Are you sure it's his?"

"What?"

He motioned toward Syl, lying unconscious on the floor. "The gun, are you sure it belongs to him?"

I told him I was.

"You're positive?"

"It was with the rest of his stuff."

Zack turned his attention back to the gun, and for a while, the only sound in the room was the soft crackle of burning wood and the slow drip of blood on the carpet.

We both stayed like that, neither of us saying a word, then Zack lifted the gun and pointed it at Syl.

I tried to say something to stop him, but it was too late. Zack pulled the trigger twice and fired two bullets into Syl's head as he slept.

34

All I wanted was to find Sara and make sure she was safe, but Zack had the gun and a different plan. He took one of the yellow blankets off Syl and tossed it to me. I used it to wrap what was left of Caroline's skull.

"Make sure it's tight," Zack said. "I don't want her leaking all over everything."

Caroline's head was a wet jumble of red and black, and I did my best not to look at it as I worked. Once I got the blanket in place, I put my hands under her head and lifted her up from the table.

It felt like lifting a bag of ice cubes and Jell-O.

When I got her upright, a wave of blood ran down her back to the floor. I jumped out of the way, and Caroline's body fell forward, hitting the table and sliding sideways off the chair to the ground.

"What the hell are you doing?" Zack motioned toward Caroline, then pointed at me. "Stop fucking around. We have to get both of them out of here and start cleaning. We don't have all damn night."

I looked down at Caroline, lying sideways on the floor, and felt my stomach cramp. For a second, I thought I was going to be sick, but I closed my eyes and focused on my breathing until the feeling passed.

Once it was gone, all that was left was the pain building behind my eyes and a voice in the back of my head telling me that I'd got exactly what I'd asked for, and now I'd get exactly what I deserved.

I had a feeling the voice was right.

I knelt down and rolled Caroline onto her back. The blood was already soaking through the blanket, and it took all my willpower to pick her up.

I put my hands under her arms and lifted her into a sitting position. I started to tell Zack to grab her legs when the bells over the office door chimed.

Zack and I both turned toward the sound.

We heard someone kicking snow off his shoes, then Butch's voice say, "You were right, Minnesota. You weren't the last one to—"

He came through the door with his notebook in one hand and his jacket in the other. When he saw us, he stopped and stared.

I tried to imagine what we looked like, hovering over the bodies, both of us covered in blood and firelight.

For a moment, no one spoke, then Butch took one tentative step forward. He looked from me to Caroline then over to Zack.

"You dumb motherfucker."

"Now hold on a minute," Zack said. "There's a good reason for this, so just—"

Butch moved fast.

Zack was still kneeling over Syl's body when Butch came across the room and kicked him in the chest. It didn't seem to do much damage, but it was an impressive kick for someone that old. I had a feeling if Butch had been twenty or thirty years younger, Zack would've been lying on the ground, too scared to get up.

"What the fuck did you do?"

Zack didn't respond, just stayed where he was and listened to Butch yell.

"We had everything set, and you go and fuck it all up. Well, I'm not going to help you out of this one, not this time." Butch pointed at him. "You can fix this one on your own."

"I'm not asking for your help."

"That's good." Butch looked at me. "I guess you got this fucking guy to help. Maybe you'll both wind up in the same prison."

"No one's going to prison," Zack said. "Not if we hurry and clean all—"

Butch reached out and slapped Zack on the side of the head. It connected hard, and I flinched at the sound.

This time, the look on Zack's face shifted, grew dark.

Butch slapped him again, harder.

I saw Zack's hand move toward the gun in his belt, but he stopped halfway and let it drop.

"You think the Cormans are gonna volunteer their pigs again?" Butch asked. "You really think they'll put their necks out for us this time?"

"They'll help."

Butch pointed at Caroline. "This ain't no goddamn truck stop whore no one's gonna miss, boy."

Zack kept quiet.

"Do you understand what I'm telling you?"

"They'll help," Zack said.

Butch's hand went up again, and this time Zack reached for the gun in his belt and pulled it out. He didn't point it at Butch, he didn't have to. Seeing it was enough.

Butch lowered his hand, slow.

"You got no idea what kind of shit you're in," Butch said. "What the hell were you thinking?"

"I had a good reason."

"I can't wait to hear it," Butch said. "While you're at it, tell me what you're going to do when her husband comes looking for her."

"Her husband?"

"That's right," Butch said. "Don't you think he might notice she ain't around anymore?"

Zack looked at me and for the first time I thought I saw doubt in his eyes. Then it was gone.

"God has a plan," he said. "All this'll work out."

Butch stepped closer.

Zack flinched.

"God's plan?" Butch said. "Are you fucking crazy? God doesn't have a plan for you."

"You're wrong."

"Boy, you are nose-deep in a sea of shit, and the only option you got is to start swallowing. If you think God is going to help you fix this mess then you're out of your fucking head."

"He's given us a way out."

"We had a way out. We had our share of that money. That was our way out. What do we have now?"

Zack looked at me and smiled.

"Now we have it all."

———

We carried Syl out first.

I had his shoulders and Zack took his feet and we followed Butch around the office to the shed behind the building. It was still snowing, but the storm had passed and the clouds had split and the sky was clear and deep. There was a full moon sitting low on the horizon, turning everything a cold silvery-blue.

"I need to check on Sara."

"We're going there next," Zack said. "You got the money in the room somewhere?"

I had no intention of letting Zack have the money, but as long as he had the gun, I was going to play along.

I told him we did.

This seemed to make him happy, and we didn't talk again until we got to the shed.

This time, the door was locked.

Zack and I stood outside while Butch fumbled with the combination. After watching him struggle for a few minutes, Zack had enough and dropped Syl's legs into the snow.

"Let me do it."

Butch stepped aside and Zack took the lock and started turning the wheel.

I eased Syl down to the ground.

"That's not the combination," Butch said.

"Sure it is. It's always been the same."

While they argued, I backed away. When I put enough distance between us, I turned and ran through the snow and around the corner.

Zack yelled after me, then I heard Butch say, "Christ, boy, stop hollering. Where's he gonna go?"

Of course, he was right.

I wasn't going anywhere.

———

Once I got to our room, I fumbled through my pockets for the key. There was no light coming through the window, and no sounds from behind the door. I wanted to believe that Sara was lying in bed, asleep, but I knew better.

I found the key and went inside.

The room was dark and empty.

I stayed in the doorway and didn't move.

The mattress had been pulled off the bed.

The suitcase was gone.

I stepped inside then crossed the room to the bathroom and pushed the door open. Sara wasn't there. I stood for a moment, listening to the slow drip of the faucet, then turned around and walked to the table.

I stood by the window and tried to think.

The first thing I needed to do was find Sara.

Caroline had said she was with Megan, but I didn't know which room she was in. And since Zack had Syl's gun, it didn't seem smart to go wandering around in plain sight.

But I didn't see any other choice.

I got up and moved toward the door.

I heard a low rumbling sound somewhere in the distance, and I stopped to listen. It was quiet at first, then it grew louder until there was no doubt what it was.

The plows were coming.

35

I stood in the doorway for a while and looked out at the parking lot. When I was sure no one was around, I stepped out onto the walkway.

I thought Megan's room was on the other side of the motel, but I had to find the right one. There were several cars parked on that side, all covered with snow. There was no way to tell which one was Megan's, so my only option was to work my way over and look for signs of life.

I ran across the parking lot to Zack's room then around the corner to the back of the building. I wanted to stay out of sight as much as possible, but that meant fighting my way through deep snow.

I could do it, but it was going to be slow.

I ran the gap between Zack's building and the next one over without a problem, but to get to the rooms on the other side of the motel, I'd have to cross in front of the playground. If anyone was watching, they'd see me.

My legs didn't want to move.

I stuck my head around the corner and looked out toward the office at the far end of the lot. There were shadows moving out front. Beyond them, I saw several yellow and blue flashing lights as the snowplows crawled their way up the highway.

I could taste something thick and sour in the back of my throat and I swallowed hard against it, then I pushed off and ran as fast as I could across the parking lot to the other building.

I'd made it almost the entire way when my foot hit one of the cement parking barriers under the snow and I fell forward, striking my head against the side of the building.

For an instant there was nothing but blackness, then a blaze of white light exploded behind my eyes and burned all the way through me. I tried to get to my feet, but the world spun around me and I couldn't tell which way was up or down.

I sat for a moment and tried to get my bearings. Once I did, I managed to crawl around to the back of the building and collapse into the snow.

I heard someone laugh in the distance, then Zack's voice say, "We could use some help over here, Nate, when you're done playing around."

Then more laughter.

I stayed on my back and stared up at a sea of silver stars and thought about Sara and the baby. A few minutes later, I heard the plows pass in front of the motel.

The road was clear.

The highway was open.

It was enough to get me going again.

I leaned against the side of the building and pushed myself to my feet. When I was standing, something warm and wet ran down the side of my face. I reached up and touched it, even though I knew what it was.

My blood looked black in the moonlight.

I walked the length of the building, ignoring the new shock of pain in my head. When I got to the end, I looked around the corner at the office.

Zack was holding Caroline's body by the shoulders and trying to back out of the door. The blanket I'd wrapped around her head had started to unravel and was now dragging along the ground.

Zack was saying something to Butch, but I couldn't hear what. Then Butch yelled, "Just do it, goddamn it."

A moment later, they were outside.

Zack dragged Caroline out, then he stopped and waited for Butch to close the office door. They were talking back and forth, and the conversation looked tense. Eventually, Butch waved him off and picked up Caroline's feet and they both started moving around the building to the shed.

I walked around to the front, still balancing myself against the building, and crossed the walkway to the window. There was no light between the curtains and no sounds from inside. I moved to the next room.

Still nothing.

"Caroline?"

The voice sounded panicked.

I ducked low then pushed myself into a shadow, as close to the building as I could get.

I saw Marcus come out of one of the rooms across the parking lot. He wasn't wearing a jacket, and the way he moved through the snow made me think he wasn't wearing shoes, either.

"Oh my God, Caroline!"

Butch and Zack stopped, and I saw Butch say something to Zack, who was holding up his hands in a calming gesture and moving toward Marcus.

"What happened to her?" Marcus was yelling. "What the hell did you do to her?"

"Now, settle down," Zack said.

Behind him, Butch yelled, "Zack, come on, don't!"

But it was too late.

Zack reached for Syl's gun in his belt then pointed it at Marcus and fired once.

The bullet struck Marcus in the throat, and a spray of blood tore out behind him in a dark mist that hung in the cold air before dissolving in the moonlight. A second later, the snow turned dark around him, and he dropped.

Zack stepped closer.

Marcus was twitching on the ground, trying to roll over. His glasses had come off one ear and now hung sideways across his face. The thin silver frames reflected clean and white in the moonlight as he struggled to crawl away.

Zack stood over him, watching, then he lifted the gun and fired.

This time, Marcus stopped moving.

— — —

Butch went crazy.

He came across the parking lot, fast, yelling, fists swinging.

Zack backed away, but Butch kept coming. I didn't hear everything he said, but it wasn't hard to put together. Butch had seen enough.

He was finished.

After tearing into Zack for a while, he walked back to the office and slammed the door behind him.

Zack called after him a couple times, but when he got no answer, he turned and started kicking Caroline's body again and again. Even from where I sat, I could hear her ribs cracking, one after the other.

Once he'd calmed down, he picked her up by the shoulders and dragged her through the snow to the shed behind the building.

I watched all of this from the shadows.

When he was gone, I looked out at Marcus lying facedown in the parking lot. He was curled in on himself and surrounded by a dark swell, while a galaxy of new snow dropped soft and slow around him.

I couldn't stop staring.

It wasn't until I saw Zack come back that I realized how much time I'd wasted. It made me wonder how bad I'd hurt my head when I fell.

I stayed where I was and didn't move.

Zack walked out to the center of the parking lot and looked down at Marcus, then he glanced up and scanned the parking lot. "Nate?"

I kept quiet.

"I better find what I'm after in your room," he said. "If I don't, things are going to be bad for you."

He stood there awhile longer.

At one point I thought he saw me crouched in the shadow against the building, but then he turned away and headed for my room.

It was time to move.

36

The next two rooms I checked were dark, so I kept moving down the row of buildings. When I got to the last one, I noticed a slip of gold light showing between the curtains and I could hear someone talking inside.

I knelt down and tried to look through the break in the curtains. At first, all I saw was the corner of the bed and a candle burning on the nightstand, then someone passed in front of the window.

I stepped back and knocked on the glass.

A second later, the curtains parted and Megan looked out. When she saw me she turned and said, "It's Nate."

I saw Sara behind her. She'd been crying.

The curtain closed.

I moved toward the door.

When I did, I saw Zack coming up the walkway. He had the gun aimed at my head, and he was close enough to where he wouldn't miss if I tried to run.

"Where is it?"

He kept walking toward me, not slowing, then he grabbed the front of my jacket and slammed the butt of the gun against the side of my head.

I never saw it coming.

A shower of orange sparks tore through my vision, and I dropped to one knee. When I looked up, Zack was standing over me. His mouth was moving, but there was no sound, only a high screaming whine.

Then, slowly, his voice started to cut through.

"Answer me, motherfucker!"

I tried to speak, but nothing came out.

Zack raised the gun to hit me again, then the door opened and I heard Megan's voice. "What the hell are you doing?"

Zack pointed the gun at her and her eyes went wide.

She backed into the room.

Sara was inside, and when she saw me she ignored the gun and ran toward me. Zack moved to stop her, but she pushed past him and knelt next to me. I must've looked pretty bad because she started crying immediately.

"Nate, my God, what happened?"

I didn't answer.

I couldn't answer.

Zack stood back and pointed the gun at us and said, "Get inside, now."

Megan inched closer then bent down and helped Sara move me inside. Things were spinning all around me, but overall, I didn't feel too bad once I sat down.

Sara turned to Zack and said, "What the hell is wrong with you?"

Zack ignored her. "Where is it?"

I heard Megan moving around in the bathroom. When she came out, she was carrying a wet washcloth. She handed it to me then looked at Zack and said, "Where is what?"

I touched the washcloth to my head, then Sara took it and started wiping away streaks of blood. She was still crying, but her eyes looked clear.

"The money," Zack said. "Where is it?"

Megan looked at me, then at Sara and shook her head. "I swear I don't know what the hell you're talking about." She looked past him. "Where's Caroline? Why are you—"

Zack turned and swung.

His fist connected with Megan's jaw, solid and hard. She fell backward and landed on the floor next to the bed.

I tried to stand.

Sara grabbed my arm and pulled me back.

"Nate, don't."

Zack looked at us and smiled. "All a big fucking game to you people, isn't it? Well, I know what you're doing, and I'm not going to fall for it. You've got it here somewhere."

He walked to the other side of the room, opening drawers and kicking over chairs, muttering to himself.

I looked at Sara and whispered, "Is it here?"

She nodded. "I'm sorry. She made me."

Zack slammed one of the drawers then turned and looked under the bed. When he stood up, he had Syl's black suitcase. He carried it to the dresser then set it on top and looked at us. "This is it, isn't it?"

No one said anything.

Zack turned back to the bag. He unzipped the top then pulled back the flap.

He stood for a moment, silent, then said, "Holy shit."

Sara reached for my hand. "Nate?"

Megan had pushed herself into a sitting position next to the bed. She was making a soft clicking sound in her throat, and didn't seem interested in anything that was happening. There was a bright red welt forming on the side of her jaw, and a thin line of blood ran down her chin and dripped on her shirt. She noticed, then reached up and touched her lip with her fingertip.

"Megan?"

She didn't look up.

I started moving toward her, but Sara grabbed me again and wouldn't let go.

This time I pulled my arm away and said, "I have to see if she's okay."

Sara shook her head.

At first I didn't understand, then I looked over at Megan sitting beside the bed. Something had shifted in her eyes, and I felt my skin turn cold.

"Lilith?"

She looked up at me and I knew.

Syl hadn't been delirious. He'd tried to tell me, but I hadn't listened. The ransacked rooms, the broken fingers, all of it.

I didn't want to believe it.

Sara squeezed my hand and said, "Can you run?"

I told her I could, and hoped it was true. I felt sturdy enough, but that might change once I stood up.

"Be ready," she said.

I went over everything Syl had said, and I cursed myself for being stupid and writing him off.

I should've known.

Zack was still standing in front of the suitcase and passing his hand over the money when Megan reached under the pillow and came out with a gun.

I had just enough time to register the silencer on the barrel and think, Just like Syl's, before she was on her feet and firing.

Even though I knew it was coming, I wasn't prepared for how fast she moved.

The first bullet came with a whisper and caught Zack on the side of his face, tearing away a chunk of his cheek and spraying blood across the suitcase and the money.

Something hit the wall then dropped to the floor by Zack's feet. When I looked, I saw two broken and bloody teeth lying on the thin motel carpet.

I couldn't look away.

The next bullet would've caught him in the head, but Zack dropped and dove toward the bathroom. The wall above him exploded in shards of plaster and dust that choked the air white.

Sara took my hand and pulled me toward the open door. Megan let us go. She was focused on Zack.

Then we were outside, running through the snow.

The pain in my head was electric, and I could feel it radiating down my spine with each step. I still had Sara's hand, and I could hear her breathing as we ran.

When we got to the end of the building, Sara slowed down. I turned and saw her looking toward the office and Marcus's body, lying in the snow.

I reached for her arm. "Don't look, come on."

"Nate, he's—"

I pulled again, harder this time, and it seemed to bring her back. We left Marcus lying in the snow and ran toward the playground at the end of the lot.

When Sara saw where we were going, she said, "No, the car. We have to get to the car."

"We can hide," I said. "She just wants the money. She'll take it and leave."

I don't think Sara agreed, but she trusted me, and she followed me the rest of the way to the playground. When we got there we crawled under the turtle slide and waited.

We didn't wait long.

I sat up on my knees and looked out over the parking lot through the slot in the turtle's shell. At first, everything was quiet, then I saw Zack come out of the room.

He staggered a bit, then walked out into the snow. He'd gone about ten feet before two tiny sprays of blood blew out from his chest and he dropped to his knees.

A moment later, Megan came outside. But this was no longer Megan. Everything about her had changed. She was a different person, the way she walked, the way she moved, all of it.

This was Lilith.

I watched her stand under the walkway and adjust Syl's suitcase in her left hand, then she crossed into the parking lot and went straight for Zack.

There was no hesitation.

When she got close, she raised the gun and fired.

Zack's head opened onto the snow and he fell forward.

"What's happening?" Sara asked.

I held up my hand, stopping her.

Lilith stood over Zack for a moment longer, then she looked up and scanned the parking lot and the buildings.

I waited for her to get in the car and go, but instead, she looked down and started searching for something on the ground.

"Nate, what's going on?"

"I don't know," I said. "She's looking for something."

"What?"

I shook my head and watched.

Lilith took several steps toward her room then turned and walked back out to the parking lot. She was still searching the ground as she went, then she stopped and lifted her head.

She was staring directly at the playground.

All at once, I understood.

She'd been looking for footprints in the snow.

And she'd found them.

37

"Is she coming?"

Lilith started across the parking lot toward the playground. She never took her eyes off the slide.

"Nate?"

There was panic in her voice, so I turned around and said, "We need to get out of here."

"No." She looked past me. "Are you sure?"

When I didn't answer, Sara moaned and pushed herself back against the edge of the shell. She tucked her legs into her chest then buried her head behind her knees and began whispering to herself.

It sounded like a prayer.

I tried to think.

We could run toward one of the buildings, or maybe north through the field, but I knew once we were out in the open, we'd be a target.

There were no good options.

I looked at Sara. She didn't have a coat, and she was shivering. I unzipped my jacket and said, "Here, take this."

Sara reached for the coat. "She's coming, isn't she?"

"Just put this on and don't make a sound."

"Why is she doing this?"

I got up and looked out through the slot toward the parking lot. Lilith was close. She still had the suitcase, and when she got to the edge of the playground, she lifted the gun and aimed at the slide.

I turned and jumped on top of Sara, pushing her down into the snow. There was a series of metallic clanks and the whisper of air, then several bullets tore through the turtle shell, splintering the plastic.

Sara screamed.

I squeezed her under me, trying to shield her with my body. A second later, several more bullets came through. This time I felt a dull thud on the back of my arm and up to my shoulder, then a deep burn.

Sara was still screaming. I wanted to tell her I was sorry, that all of this was my fault, but nothing came out.

More bullets buzzed past us, hitting the ground and spraying snow and dirt into the air. I could feel blood running over my shoulder and soaking into my shirt.

I closed my eyes and waited.

A second later, there was a loud crash and Sara stopped screaming. It sounded like—

A shotgun?

I opened my eyes and looked out under the edge of the shell. All I saw were Lilith's legs. She had her back to us and was facing out toward the parking lot. Beyond her, coming into the playground, I saw a pair of dirty jeans and work boots.

Lilith took a step back, staggered, then dropped the suitcase. It hit the snow by her feet and landed on its side. A moment later, Lilith's legs gave out and she fell backward into the snow. The gun flew from her hand and landed a few feet away.

I stared at it.

Sara was whimpering under me. I looked down and said, "Are you okay?"

She didn't answer.

I tried to push myself up, but my left arm collapsed under me and I rolled to the side and bit down hard against the pain. All I could hear was Sara's breathing and the footsteps in the snow, coming closer.

We watched the work boots stop next to the suitcase. Then we heard Butch's voice.

"Come out of there."

Neither one of us moved.

"Unless you're both dead, you'd better come out."

I eased myself over and started to crawl out. When I did, I heard Sara's breath catch in her throat.

I looked down and saw blood on the snow, then I reached back and felt my shoulder.

There was a line of torn skin where the bullet had hit, but I didn't feel a puncture wound. I was pretty sure the bullet hadn't gone in, and even though it was bleeding a lot, I knew things could've been much worse.

I was lucky.

We crawled the rest of the way out then stood up.

Butch was kneeling next to the suitcase. He had the top open and was staring at the blood-stained money inside. When he saw us, he zipped the flap and stood up.

He kept the shotgun at his waist, pointed at us.

A few feet away, Lilith was lying on her side in the snow. When Sara saw her, she put one hand to her mouth and turned away.

Lilith wasn't dead, but the left side of her chest had been torn open from her armpit to her waist, and the snow around her was wet and still in the moonlight. I could hear her talking, but her voice was soft and the words were lost.

For a moment, no one moved.

Butch stared at us, then he motioned to my shoulder and said, "She got you."

"Yeah." My voice cracked. "She did."

Lilith's eyes were moving from the left to the right, but I could tell they weren't seeing anything. She'd stopped talking, and now the only sound she made came from deep in her throat, wet and choking.

I saw the gun lying a few feet away in the snow.

I thought if I moved fast enough—

"All this is your damn fault," Butch said. "You two brought a hell of a mess with you."

Sara was leaning against me, crying.

Neither of us spoke.

"Zack was a wreck of a human being, but he was the only family I had left." He looked down at Lilith. "Now he's dead."

I took half a step toward the gun.

Butch didn't seem to notice.

"Goddamn it, I never killed anyone in my life," he said. "Not even in the war. I was always proud of that."

I took another step but this time Butch saw me and raised the gun to his shoulder.

Sara screamed and dug her nails into my arm.

I held my hands up in front of me and said, "Wait, you don't have to do this."

Butch stared at me down the twin barrels of the shotgun and said, "No choice."

"There's always a choice."

"Not this time," Butch said. "Two more bodies ain't gonna make a bit of difference."

"No, we can all just walk away from this," I said. "We're not going to say a word to anyone."

Butch shook his head. "That'd be easy for you, wouldn't it? You didn't kill anyone, so now you want to walk away while I go to jail."

Lilith coughed and I felt Sara let go of my arm.

I stayed between her and Butch.

"You won't go to jail," I said. "We're not going to say anything."

"I can't risk it."

We looked at each other for a moment, silent, then I pointed at the shotgun and said, "You've only got one shell left. You'll have to reload to get us both."

Butch didn't speak.

"One of us will get to that gun before you do."

The expression on Butch's face changed, turned dark, then he smiled. It wasn't a good smile.

I started to tell him again that we didn't have to do this, that we could work something out, when I heard Lilith gasp and saw Butch's eyes shift past me.

"Hey, goddamn it." He moved to the side and pointed the gun. "Don't do it. Put it down, now!"

I turned and saw Sara crouched next to Lilith. When she stood, she had the gun in her hand.

Butch's finger tightened on the trigger.

"No!" I moved fast, stepping in front of him, blocking the shot. "She's pregnant."

Butch looked at me, and for an instant something changed in his eyes, then it was gone. I moved toward him, fast, thinking I had a chance of knocking the gun away before he could fire. When I did, I heard a familiar, metallic whisper of air behind me, then another.

Then nothing.

Butch stood for a moment, staring past me, then he lowered the gun, slow.

I turned around.

Sara was standing over Lilith. She had the gun pointed down at her, and a new swell of blood was pooling into the snow around her head.

The soft choking sounds had stopped.

For a while, no one moved.

"Sara?"

She looked at me, but there was nothing there, no emotion at all.

I started to say something else, but Sara moved away from Lilith and walked past me toward Butch. When she got close to him, he stepped back.

Sara held the gun out to him.

"Take it."

Butch hesitated, then reached out and took the gun.

"Now you didn't kill anyone."

Butch looked at the gun, then over at Lilith. I thought he was going to say something, but before he could, the lights around the walkways buzzed and lit up. The main highway sign outside the office flickered into a large neon Palm Tree with the words the oasis inn and vacancy underneath.

Butch looked around then back at me.

"Power's back."

The casual tone wasn't what I'd expected, and all I could do was agree. I asked, "What do you want us to do?"

He didn't say anything right away, then he pocketed Lilith's gun and said, "I want you to get the hell out of here. I've got a few phone calls to make before the sheriff decides to stop by and check in."

I felt like I should say something else, but before I could, Sara grabbed my hand and started pulling me away. As we passed the suitcase, I leaned down to pick it up.

Butch stopped me.

"Leave it," he said. This time his voice was cold.

I hesitated, only for an instant, but it was long enough to see Butch lift the shotgun, just a bit.

Sara pulled on my arm, hard. "Nate, come on."

I took one last look at the suitcase then turned and followed Sara out of the playground toward our room.

The bags were sitting inside the door. Zack had torn through them when he'd come looking for the money, but it didn't take long to put everything back together and load them in the car.

We moved as fast as we could, and five minutes later, we pulled out of the motel parking lot and onto the highway.

Neither of us said a word for a long time.

Part III

Part III

38

We made it to Omaha just before sunrise.

I found a twenty-four-hour SaveMore off the interstate and I pulled into the parking lot and stopped under a streetlight. It was snowing, and the parking lot was almost totally empty.

"Is this place open?" Sara asked.

I pointed to the open 24 hours sign above the door, then gave Sara a list of things to buy. Once she went inside, I leaned my seat back and closed my eyes.

It wasn't much of a rest, but it helped.

When she came out, she had a plastic shopping bag filled with sterile gauze, rubbing alcohol, and antibiotic ointment.

"Is this going to work?"

I told her it would.

We got back on the interstate and drove through town. I wanted to find someplace outside the city where I could get cleaned up and grab something to eat.

To the east, a thin slice of light ran pink along the horizon, and by the time we were out of the city, the sky was a burning twist of orange and red.

"How about there?" Sara pointed at a large red neon sign. "Sapp Brothers. Is that a truck stop?"

The sign was shaped like a giant coffee percolator.

It made me think of Caroline and Marcus.

"Yeah," I said. "It is."

———

I stood over the sink and watched the swirl of blood circle down the drain, then I looked at my shoulder in the mirror and examined the bandage.

It wasn't the best patch job, but it would do.

I took a clean shirt out of my bag and slipped it over my head then down past my shoulder. I'd managed to wash most of the blood off my face and hands, but I could still feel it in my hair and under my clothes.

I hoped it was my blood, but I wasn't sure.

I stayed in the bathroom for a while longer, staring at the bags under my eyes and the tiny cuts on my face from the plastic shrapnel under the slide. When I was ready, I picked up the gauze and the rubbing alcohol and put them back in the Save-More bag, then I turned and walked out of the bathroom and into the diner.

There was a row of newspaper boxes by the front door. One of them had the *Chicago Tribune.* I dropped in a few quarters, then opened the front and grabbed a copy.

When I got back to the booth, Sara was sitting there, staring out the window. Our food had come while I'd been in the bathroom, but it didn't look like she'd eaten any of hers.

I dropped the paper on the table and sat down.

Sara didn't look at me.

"You should eat," I said.

"Not hungry."

I kept quiet.

If she didn't want to eat, it was her choice. There wasn't a thing I could do to make her.

But I was starving.

I picked up my fork and cut into the eggs and hash browns on my plate. They were hot and greasy and absolutely delicious. I ate them all in five bites then finished what was left of my coffee.

I was starting to feel alive again.

"You sure you don't want to eat?"

Sara looked down at her food then pushed the plate across the table toward me. "You can have it."

"You need to eat."

Sara shook her head. "I can't stand to look at food right now. Go ahead."

I didn't argue.

When I finished, I reached for the paper and scanned through the local stories. On page three I saw an article about a real estate developer named Rodney McGee who'd been murdered at his house in Hyde Park.

According to the article, Rodney had made a fortune through questionable business deals. He'd also had strong ties to organized crime, so no one was surprised when he turned up dead.

But the actual focus of the article had to do with his wife, Lilith McGee, who was still missing.

The paper didn't have much on her.

They knew she'd been born in St. Petersburg and had immigrated to the United States almost five years ago. They could find no records of her life in Russia, other than a short period of military service. All they had to go on were the couple's friends who told the *Tribune* that Lilith and Rodney met while he was in Russia on business, and that she moved back to the States to marry him.

Most people who knew them believed if she wasn't dead, then she had something to do with his murder.

I read the entire article twice.

There was no mention of Syl or the missing money.

When I closed the paper, I debated telling Sara. In the end, I decided not to.

I wanted her to forget, even though I knew she never would.

I reached for the coffeepot on the table and refilled my cup then said, "If we go nonstop, we can make it to Salt Lake City tonight, then Reno tomorrow."

Sara was quiet.

"It'll be a push, and we won't have a lot of time to rest once we get to Nevada, but we can do it."

Sara whispered something I didn't quite hear.

I asked her to say it again.

"I said what kind of people are we?"

"What do you mean?"

She shook her head. "Forget it."

I pushed, and after a while she gave in.

"Don't you feel responsible for what happened?"

"We didn't kill anyone."

"I did."

"She wanted to kill us," I said. "She was going to kill us. Butch was going to kill us. You did the right thing."

My voice came out louder than I thought it would, and I noticed the couple at the next table look up briefly, then back down at their plates.

"No, I didn't," she said. "We didn't."

"I don't want to talk about it here."

"Butch was right," she said. "It was our fault. We brought it with us, like a curse."

"Sara, stop."

"What kind of people are we, Nate?"

I turned and waved to our waitress then picked up my coffee and finished it.

"God isn't going to let us get away with this." There were tears on her face. "We're going to have to answer for what we've done."

The waitress came by and asked if we needed anything else. I told her we didn't and she set the ticket on the table then took the empty plates.

When she was gone, I leaned toward Sara and said, "What do you want me to do about it now?"

"Just admit it," she said. "Admit that it was our fault, that we're the reason all those people are dead."

"I can't do that."

"Why not?"

"Because Zack was a crazy fuck, that's why." I looked at the couple at the next table and they looked back. When I spoke again, I fought to keep my voice quiet. "He was a tweaker and he was out of his mind and that's why all those people are dead, not because of us."

"We could've stopped him."

"How?"

"We could've done something," she said. "But we didn't."

I didn't know what to say to that, so I didn't say anything. Instead, I got up and grabbed our ticket then walked to the front of the restaurant and paid.

Something about what she'd said burned in me, but I pushed it away and tried to forget.

When I looked back, Sara was staring out the window at the highway and the line of cars moving west toward the horizon. I watched her for a long time. When I went back to the table, I sat across from her and reached out for her hands.

She didn't want to give them to me at first, but eventually she did.

"You didn't do anything wrong," I said. "You saved our lives."

Sara looked at me but all I saw in her face was sadness. She let go of my hands, and when she spoke again, her voice was soft.

"I didn't do it for us."

Reno

39

It was a long drop.

I eased my way toward the edge, then took a couple nails from my belt and picked up another shingle. The sun was low on the horizon, but the air was hot. I could feel the lines of sweat rolling over my neck and down my back.

It was the greatest feeling in the world.

I finished the row then climbed to the top of the roof and looked out over the string of new houses snaking their way through the canyon. The ones closest to me were practically finished, but the farther down the line, the more work needed to be done.

I reached for another stack of shingles.

"Nate?"

I looked down and saw Hank Johansen, the foreman, looking up at me. He had his hand over his eyes, shielding them from the setting sun. The rest of the crew shuffled past him on their way out to their cars.

I'd lost track of time.

"Come on down," Hank said. "I need to see you in my office before you take off."

I waved, then set the shingles back on the stack and walked to the ladder on the opposite side of the roof. When I climbed down, I stopped by the cooler for a drink of water, then I crossed the road toward Hank's office.

The office was a white trailer parked on the far end of the job site. There were two desks inside and four filing cabinets. In one corner, an oscillating fan pushed hot air from one end of the room to the other.

Hank was standing at one of the filing cabinets when I walked in. He had a folder in his hand, and when he saw me he used it to point to a metal folding chair.

"Have a seat."

I did.

Hank went behind his desk and sat down. "How do you like Reno so far?"

"I love it."

"Heat's not getting to you?"

"Can't get enough of it."

"Wait until July," he said. "You might have a different opinion."

I told him he might be right, but I knew he wasn't.

The hotter the better.

"Listen, Nate. I want to tell you how much I appreciate all you've done these past few weeks. You're a hell of a hard worker."

I thanked him.

"So this is tough for me, but I'm going to have to let you go." He sat back in his chair. "Believe me, I don't want to do it, but with the way the market is nowadays, I just don't have the work."

I wasn't shocked, but at the same time I felt something heavy settle at the base of my stomach.

"The market?"

"Afraid so, and since you're the low man on the totem pole around here . . ." He paused. "In a perfect world, there would be two or three guys I'd like to see go before you, but that's just not the way it works."

I told him I understood.

"I hope you do." He opened the folder then took a piece of paper and a pen from his desk and started to write. "Here's a name and a number for one of the foremen over at Orin Construction. Talk to Ben and tell him I sent you. I'll give him a call tomorrow and tell him to keep an eye out for you. Can't promise what he'll say, but I'll do what I can to get you on over there."

He finished writing then handed me the paper.

"I appreciate it."

"We'll keep your name on file, too," he said. "Once things change, I'll make sure to give you a call."

I nodded then got up to leave.

"Real sorry about this, Nate."

"Yeah," I said. "Me, too."

———

I wasn't ready to go home, so I stopped by the Washoe County Library and sorted through the periodicals until I found the *Chicago Tribune.* The library only got the Sunday edition, and it was always late, but I'd made a point of coming by and reading it every week.

At first, the story of Rodney and Lilith McGee was big news, but eventually it faded from the first section to smaller articles buried in the back of the paper.

Today, there was nothing at all.

It was a good sign.

A few weeks earlier, I'd found another article in the *Des Moines Register*. This one mentioned a motel fire forty miles south of Frieberg.

According to the report, the blaze started when an unchecked candle was placed too close to a set of curtains. Then, with the help of the wind, the fire spread from one building to the next, destroying the entire property.

No fatalities were listed.

The next week, I went back and searched the *Register* for more news, but there was no mention of the fire.

The motel was forgotten.

I stood up and walked to the window and looked out at the city lights hovering brown and dull in the dry air.

Even at night, Reno looked dirty.

After a while, I put the paper back in the rack then took the stairs to the main level and walked out to my car. I still didn't feel like going home, but I knew I had to. Sara was probably worried.

I got in the car and started the engine.

Somewhere, a dog barked.

I decided to take the long way home.

40

The afternoon we got to Reno, we drove to my cousin's house. He looked happy to see us, even set us up in a spare room, but once we were alone, Sara told me he was nervous about us staying there.

I told her she was imagining things.

Turned out, she wasn't.

After the first few days, it became obvious my cousin's wife didn't want us in her house. Sara and I would hear them fighting about it at night, and the more they fought, the more I realized she wanted us to hear.

Luckily, I'd found a job roofing houses. It paid cash every day, so it didn't take long before we had enough money to get our own place. By then, things had gone bad at my cousin's house, and we couldn't get out fast enough.

We found a furnished basement apartment on the outskirts of downtown Reno. The building was old and the pipes rattled and ran brown for the first few days, but it was clean and cheap and for a while we thought things could be good again.

Now, I was out of work.

Sara wasn't going to be happy.

———

There was no place to park at our building, so each night I had to circle the block until I found a space. This time, I got lucky and found a spot at the end of the street.

I parked and walked the rest of the way home. When I got close, I could see our apartment window flickering blue along the base of the building, and I knew what I'd find inside.

I was right.

Sara was lying on the couch watching TV. She had on the same clothes she'd slept in the night before, and her hair was dirty and pulled back in a loose ponytail.

When I came through the door, she looked up at me and said, "Hey, baby."

"How are you feeling?"

"About the same."

I set my tools on the floor next to the door, then kicked off my work boots and joined her on the couch.

For a while, we didn't speak.

There was a nature show on TV about a wasp that paralyzes a spider then lays her eggs inside its body.

Sara wasn't watching.

She was somewhere else.

"Did you eat today?" I asked.

"A little."

I wasn't sure I believed her, but there wasn't much I could

say about it either. I knew she tried to eat. She just couldn't keep anything down.

"Do you want to go talk to that doctor again?"

"What for? You heard what he said. The first trimester is the worst. It'll get better."

"Is that the problem?"

Sara closed her eyes. "Nate, stop."

I wanted to push, but I didn't.

Nothing I had to say was going to help.

I sat for a while longer then got up and went into the kitchen and looked through the cabinets. All I could find to eat was tomato soup. I opened a can and poured it into a bowl then ran it through the microwave.

When it was hot, I carried it out to the living room and set it on the coffee table.

"You didn't have to do that," Sara said.

"You need to eat."

She pushed herself up then leaned forward and stirred the soup. "I don't know."

"Just try it."

Sara lifted the spoon halfway, smelled it, then dropped it back in the bowl. "I can't. I'm sorry."

For a while we were both quiet, then Sara looked at me and said, "Do you ever think God is punishing us?"

"No, I never think that."

"Why not?"

"Because if there is a God, I like to think he'd be above revenge."

Sara looked at me for a moment then turned back to the TV. "I think he's punishing us. I think we're cursed."

"Jesus, Sara."

"That's what I think," she said.

I could feel the anger building in my chest.

I swallowed it, then grabbed the bowl and walked back to the kitchen and dumped the soup in the sink. I stood for a while and watched the red swirl disappear down the drain, then I rinsed the bowl and put it upside down to dry.

When I went back to the living room, Sara was lying on the couch with her eyes closed. I sat next to her and brushed the hair away from her face. She looked up at me then moved her head to my lap.

After a while, she was asleep.

On TV, the eggs hatched and the tiny wasps ate the spider alive.

I closed my eyes and thought about God.

41

In the dream I was sitting on a deserted beach, staring out at a silver reflection of sunlight on a clear blue sea. The ocean breeze was warm and sweet and as gentle as a kiss, and when I closed my eyes I felt like I was floating.

There was a boy with me, down by the water.

He was young, a child, and his hair was an explosion of blond curls. He had a bag of breadcrumbs in one hand, and several hungry seagulls hovered over him like angels.

I knew him, but I didn't.

I watched him reach into the bag and throw a handful of bread into the air. The seagulls dove around him, and he laughed then turned and ran down the beach.

The seagulls followed.

After a while, he stopped and did it again.

Soon, he was far away.

I got up and started walking along the shore, following him. There was a thin haze hanging low over the water, and the boy seemed to fade into it.

I started walking faster, then I called out to him.

The boy stopped for a moment then raised one hand and waved. Tiny starfish fingers, opening and closing.

A child's wave.

I could feel the tension in my chest and I started to run. The boy watched me, then turned and was gone.

I kept going.

Soon the sun set and the sea faded to black. The moon, heavy and swollen, hung low on the horizon and turned the beach a cold blue. I could hear the waves rolling over the sand at my feet, but I didn't look down.

Then I saw him.

He was standing up ahead, staring at a line of dunes along the beach. He didn't see me, and when I got close, I got down on one knee and touched his arm.

The boy turned and looked at me.

For a moment, I couldn't speak.

"Vincent?"

But not Vincent.

The boy turned back to the dunes. I followed his gaze, but all I saw was sand.

I asked him what he was looking at.

He raised one hand and pointed.

At first there was nothing, then I saw them.

The dunes were alive, crawling with hundreds of tiny, struggling turtles, each one lurching through the moonlight toward the sea.

I stepped back and watched them fight through the sand until they reached the shore, then, one by one, the waves came and carried them away.

There were tears on my face, but I barely noticed. A moment later I felt a small hand on my arm.

When I looked down, the boy was gone.

———

I opened my eyes, and at first I didn't know where I was. I sat up slow, listening to the pulse behind my ears, waiting for it to slow down. Once it did, I noticed Sara wasn't in bed.

I looked at the clock: 3:15 a.m.

I pushed the covers back then got out of bed and opened the door and walked out into the living room. The apartment was dark except for a thin line of white light leaking out from under the bathroom door.

I went to the kitchen and poured a glass of water and drank it in two swallows. The dream was still vivid in my mind, but the more I thought about it, the more it faded.

I set the glass in the sink then started back to the bedroom. When I passed the bathroom door, I stopped and pressed my ear against the wood and listened.

I could hear Sara crying.

I knocked, soft.

No answer.

"Sara?"

"Nate?"

Her voice sounded thin and weak, and I felt something cold slide along the back of my neck.

"Are you okay?"

"No," she said. "Something's wrong."

I reached for the knob and opened the door.

Sara was sitting on the toilet. In the harsh fluorescent light, I could see each of her ribs through her skin. She looked up at me. Her eyes were swollen and wet.

"Sara?"

She held out her hands and I saw the blood.

"I'm bleeding."

For a second, her entire body seemed to shake, then the tears came.

"Oh, God, Nate. I'm bleeding."

42

I sat in the waiting room until the nurse came out and said, "You can come back, if you'd like." Then I got up and followed her down an empty white hallway to a room marked recovery.

"Go on in," the nurse said. "She's alone."

I opened the door.

Sara was sitting on a raised bed by a dark window. When she saw me, she looked up and tried to smile.

"How are you feeling?"

"Sad," she said. "I'm so sorry."

I sat next to her and told her there was nothing to be sorry about. For a moment, it seemed to help, then her eyes drifted and she was gone again.

"What did the doctor say?"

"Not to get discouraged, that sometimes this happens, especially the first time."

"But you're okay?"

"I want to go home," she said. "But I'm fine."

Her clothes were folded and stacked on a red plastic chair next to the bed. I picked them up and set them next to her.

"Why don't you get dressed. I'll take you home."

She stared at her clothes then up at me. "No, I mean I want to go *home*. I want to go back to Minnesota."

I didn't say anything right away.

"I don't want to be out here anymore," she said. "Especially not now."

"Can we talk about this?"

"I don't think so."

"What about us? We're getting married."

"You still want to marry me?"

I told her I did.

I told her we could have a good life together.

"We can have a good life in Minnesota."

I shook my head. "I can't go back."

She started to argue, but I didn't hear a word she was saying. All I could think about were the winters in Minnesota. The thought of being surrounded by all that snow made it hard to breathe.

"Are you okay?"

I lied and told her I was.

Sara watched me for a moment, then eased herself out of bed and started to get dressed. Neither of us talked again until we were in the car driving back to the apartment.

"I hate it here," she said. "Everything is dead."

The next two days were hard on us both. I ended up telling Sara I'd lost my job, and at first she was happy. She said it was a sign that we were meant to go back home.

I told her I wasn't going back.

She didn't understand.

I told her I'd take her to Minnesota, but I wasn't going to stay. My plan was to sell the car and buy a one-way ticket to Costa Rica or Rio.

I wanted to be someplace hot.

Someplace I could burn.

———

Our rent was paid through the end of the week, so on Saturday, I filled the Dodge with gas then packed our bags into the back end. I left most of my stuff behind in a Dumpster. There wasn't much to start with, and where I was going, I wouldn't need any of it.

Packing was easier this time.

I was able to get most of Sara's stuff in without a problem. Then, as I was loading the last few bags, I noticed something green sticking out from under the driver's seat.

I forced myself to finish packing, then walked around and opened the door and pushed the seat forward. I reached down and pulled the backpack out. I held it for a moment before closing the door and going inside.

Sara was cleaning the kitchen when I walked in. She smiled at me, then, when she saw what I was carrying, she turned away and slumped against the counter.

I sat at the kitchen table and unzipped the bag. I took out the two stacks of money and set them on the table in front of me.

"What are we going to do?"

Sara didn't say anything.

"We could use it to move," I said. "Head south, find a beach. We could be—"

Sara turned on me, fast. "No!"

I stared at her.

She looked at the money. "Get rid of it, Nate. I don't want it. I don't want any of it."

I started to ask why, but she cut me off.

"It's bad luck," she said. "It's cursed."

I held the money in my hand.

I couldn't argue with her anymore, not about that.

Sara turned back to the counter. "Just get rid of it, please?"

"What if there was a way—"

"No, Nate."

"What if we could make everything right?"

Sara looked at me. She wasn't convinced.

I started to talk.

43

We walked into the Silver Legacy casino and went straight for the cashier. I took the money and handed it to the woman working in the cage.

She looked at me and said, "How much is here?"

"Almost twenty thousand."

She stepped away from the window and picked up a phone. A few minutes later, a man came out of a back room with a stack of forms for me to sign.

When I finished, he looked at me and said, "Eighteen thousand five hundred. How do you want it?"

"What do you mean?"

"How do you want your chips?"

I looked at Sara. She shrugged.

I turned back to the man and said, "As few as possible."

He frowned then counted out a small stack of chips and slid them toward me. "You sure about that?"

I told him I was.

"We're only making one bet."

———

It was an easy solution.

One bet, one spin.

The most unlucky number there was.

Black thirteen.

If we hit it, the payoff was thirty-five to one. We'd have enough money for a lifetime on any South American beach. If we missed, the money would be gone along with the curse, and Sara would go back to Minnesota, alone.

One bet, one spin.

We walked through the bells and the flashing lights until we found the roulette tables. There were several of them, and we stood for a while, trying to decide.

"Which one?" Sara asked.

"You pick."

She walked between them, then pointed to the last table in the line and said, "How about here?"

I pulled out one of the chairs and sat down.

Sara sat next to me.

The dealer was stacking chips in the tray. When she finished, she stood back and waited. I noticed she was wearing a small, emerald green turtle pin on her vest.

I smiled.

"Bets, please."

I put all our chips on black thirteen.

The dealer reached out and counted them.

"One minute."

She turned and the pit boss came forward.

"You sure you want this bet?" he asked.

I told him I was.

He picked up a phone. When he hung up, he turned to the dealer and nodded.

"Okay, here we go," the dealer said. "Good luck."

She started the wheel moving, then placed the ball on the rim and sent it buzzing the opposite way.

We watched it go.

I turned to Sara. She was holding her breath.

"You okay?" I asked.

She looked up at me and smiled.

"Yeah," she said. "I'm okay."

For the first time in a long time, I believed her.

The pit boss walked up and stood behind the dealer. Several other people gathered around us.

We were drawing a crowd.

I leaned toward Sara and said, "Kiss me."

"What?"

"Kiss me," I said. "For good luck."

Sara frowned. "That doesn't work, Nate."

"Of course it does," I said. "It always works."

The ball slowed and the dealer waved her hand over the table and said, "No more bets."

Sara looked at me.

"Come on," I said. "Kiss me."

Sara hesitated, then leaned into me and pressed her lips against mine. When they touched, I felt it go all the way down my spine, and I never wanted to let her go.

The wheel spun, and the ball rattled to a stop.

Neither of us looked up.

It was a good kiss.

Acknowledgments

I'd like to thank my agent, Allan Guthrie, for his hard work and invaluable insight. Thanks to my U.S. editor, Eric Raab, and everyone at Tor/Forge. Thanks to my U.K. editor, Francesca Main, and everyone at Simon & Schuster. Thank you to Sean Doolittle for years of advice, encouragement, and friendship. And thank you to John Schoenfelder for getting the ball rolling. I'd also like to express my gratitude to my early readers, Eric Stark, Stephen Sommerville, Mark Edward Deloy, and Eric Smetana. Most of all, I want to thank my wife, Amy, for her love and her unwavering support, especially during those times when I forgot to tell her how much they meant to me.